THE ALEXANDER SHAKESPEARE

General Editor
R.B. Kennedy

Additional notes and editing
Mike Gould

HAMLET

William Shakespeare

COLLINS
CLASSICS

Harper Press
An imprint of HarperCollins*Publishers*
77–85 Fulham Palace Road
Hammersmith
London W6 8JB

This Harper Press paperback edition published 2011

A catalogue record for this book is available from the British Library

ISBN-13: 978-0-00-790234-7

Printed and bound in Great Britain by Clays Ltd, St Ives plc

Life & Times section © Gerard Cheshire
Introduction by Stuart Gillespie
Shakespeare: Words and Phrases adapted from
Collins English Dictionary
Typesetting in Kalix by Palimpsest Book Production Limited,
Falkirk, Stirlingshire

10 9 8 7 6 5 4 3 2 1

Prefatory Note

This Shakespeare play uses the full Alexander text. By keeping in mind the fact that the language has changed considerably in four hundred years, as have customs, jokes, and stage conventions, the editors have aimed at helping the modern reader – whether English is their mother tongue or not – to grasp the full significance of the play. The Notes, intended primarily for examination candidates, are presented in a simple, direct style. The needs of those unfamiliar with British culture have been specially considered.

Since quiet study of the printed word is unlikely to bring fully to life plays that were written directly for the public theatre, attention has been drawn to dramatic effects which are important in performance. The editors see Shakespeare's plays as living works of art which can be enjoyed today on stage, film and television in many parts of the world.

CONTENTS

An Elizabethan playhouse. Note the apron stage protruding into the auditorium, the space below it, the inner room at the rear of the stage, the gallery above the inner stage, the canopy over the main stage, and the absence of a roof over the audience.

The Theatre in Shakespeare's Day

On the face of it, the conditions in the Elizabethan theatre were not such as to encourage great writers. The public playhouse itself was not very different from an ordinary inn-yard; it was open to the weather; among the spectators were often louts, pickpockets and prostitutes; some of the actors played up to the rowdy elements in the audience by inserting their own jokes into the authors' lines, while others spoke their words loudly but unfeelingly; the presentation was often rough and noisy, with fireworks to represent storms and battles, and a table and a few chairs to represent a tavern; there were no actresses, so boys took the parts of women, even such subtle and mature ones as Cleopatra and Lady Macbeth; there was rarely any scenery at all in the modern sense. In fact, a quick inspection of the English theatre in the reign of Elizabeth I by a time-traveller from the twentieth century might well produce only one positive reaction: the costumes were often elaborate and beautiful.

Shakespeare himself makes frequent comments in his plays about the limitations of the playhouse and the actors of his time, often apologizing for them. At the beginning of *Henry V* the Prologue refers to the stage as 'this unworthy scaffold' and to the theatre building (the Globe, probably) as 'this wooden O', and emphasizes the urgent need for imagination in making up for all the deficiencies of presentation. In introducing Act IV the Chorus goes so far as to say:

> . . . we shall much disgrace
> With four or five most vile and ragged foils,
> Right ill-dispos'd in brawl ridiculous,
> The name of Agincourt, (lines 49–52)

In *A Midsummer Night's Dream* (Act V, Scene i) he seems to dismiss actors with the words:

The best in this kind are but shadows.

Yet Elizabeth's theatre, with all its faults, stimulated dramatists to a variety of achievement that has never been equalled and, in Shakespeare, produced one of the greatest writers in history. In spite of all his grumbles he seems to have been fascinated by the challenge that it presented him with. It is necessary to re-examine his theatre carefully in order to understand how he was able to achieve so much with the materials he chose to use. What sort of place was the Elizabethan playhouse in reality? What sort of people were these criticized actors? And what sort of audiences gave them their living?

The Development of the Theatre up to Shakespeare's Time

For centuries in England noblemen had employed groups of skilled people to entertain them when required. Under Tudor rule, as England became more secure and united, actors such as these were given more freedom, and they often performed in public, while still acknowledging their 'overlords' (in the 1570s, for example, when Shakespeare was still a schoolboy at Stratford, one famous company was called 'Lord Leicester's Men'). London was rapidly becoming larger and more important in the second half of the sixteenth century, and many of the companies of actors took the opportunities offered to establish themselves at inns on the main roads leading to the City (for example, the Boar's Head in Whitechapel and the Tabard in South-wark) or in the City itself. These groups of actors would come to an agreement with the inn-keeper which would give them the use of the yard for their performances after people had eaten and drunk well in the middle of the day. Before long, some inns were taken over completely by companies of players and thus became the first public theatres. In 1574 the officials of the City of London issued an order which shows clearly that these theatres were both popular and also offensive to some respectable people, because the order complains about 'the inordinate haunting of great multitudes of people, specially youth, to plays interludes and shows; namely occasion of frays and quarrels, evil practices of incontinency in great inns . . .' There is evidence that, on public holidays, the theatres on the banks of the Thames were crowded with noisy apprentices and tradesmen, but it would be wrong to think that audiences were always undiscriminating and loudmouthed. In spite of the disapproval of Puritans and the more staid members of society, by the 1590s, when Shakespeare's plays were beginning to be performed, audiences consisted of a good cross-section of English society, nobility as well as workers, intellectuals as well as simple people out for a laugh; also (and in this respect English theatres were unique in Europe), it was quite normal for respectable women to attend plays. So Shakespeare had to write plays which would appeal to people of widely different kinds. He had to provide 'something for everyone' but at the same time to take care to unify the material so that it would not seem to fall into separate pieces as they watched it. A speech like that of the drunken porter in *Macbeth* could provide the 'groundlings' with a belly-laugh, but also held a deeper significance for those who could appreciate it. The audience he wrote for was one of a number of apparent drawbacks which Shakespeare was able to turn to his and our advantage.

Shakespeare's Actors

Nor were all the actors of the time mere 'rogues, vagabonds and sturdy beggars' as some were described in a Statute of 1572. It is true that many of them had a hard life and earned very little money, but leading actors could become partners in the ownership of the theatres in which they acted: Shakespeare was a shareholder in the Globe and the Blackfriars theatres when he was an actor as well as a playwright. In any case, the attacks made on Elizabethan actors were usually directed at their morals and not at their acting ability; it is clear that many of them must have been good at their trade if they were able to interpret complex works like the great tragedies in such a way as to attract enthusiastic audiences. Undoubtedly some of the boys took the women's parts with skill and confidence, since a man called Coryate, visiting Venice in 1611, expressed surprise that women could act as well as they: 'I saw women act, a thing that I never saw before . . . and they performed it with as good a grace, action, gesture . . . as ever I saw any masculine actor.' The quality of most of the actors who first presented Shakespeare's plays is probably accurately summed up by Fynes Moryson, who wrote, '. . . as there be, in my opinion, more plays in London than in all the parts of the world I have seen, so do these players or comedians excel all other in the world.'

The Structure of the Public Theatre

Although the 'purpose-built' theatres were based on the inn-yards which had been used for play-acting, most of them were circular. The walls contained galleries on three storeys from which the wealthier patrons watched, they must have been something like the 'boxes' in a modern theatre, except that they held much larger numbers – as many as 1500. The 'groundlings' stood on the floor of the building, facing a raised stage which projected from the 'stage-wall', the main features of which were:

1 a small room opening on to the back of the main stage and on the same level as it (rear stage),
2 a gallery above this inner stage (upper stage),
3 canopy projecting from above the gallery over the main stage, to protect the actors from the weather (the 700 or 800 members of the audience who occupied the yard, or 'pit' as we call it today, had the sky above them).

In addition to these features there were dressing-rooms behind the stage and a space underneath it from which entrances could be made through trap-doors. All the acting areas – main stage, rear stage, upper stage and under stage – could be entered by actors directly from their dressing rooms, and all of them were used in productions of Shakespeare's plays. For example, the inner stage, an almost cavelike structure, would have been where Ferdinand and Miranda are 'discovered' playing chess in the last act of *The Tempest*, while the upper stage was certainly the balcony from which Romeo climbs down in Act III of *Romeo and Juliet*.

It can be seen that such a building, simple but adaptable, was not really unsuited to the presentation of plays like Shakespeare's. On the contrary, its simplicity guaranteed the minimum of distraction, while its shape and construction must have produced a sense of involvement on the part of the audience that modern producers would envy.

Other Resources of the Elizabethan Theatre

Although there were few attempts at scenery in the public theatre (painted backcloths were occasionally used in court performances), Shakespeare and his fellow playwrights were able to make use of a fair variety of 'properties', lists of such articles have survived: they include beds, tables, thrones, and also trees, walls, a gallows, a Trojan horse and a 'Mouth of Hell'; in a list of properties belonging to the manager, Philip Henslowe, the curious item 'two mossy banks' appears. Possibly one of them was used for the

> bank whereon the wild thyme blows,
> Where oxlips and the nodding violet grows

in *A Midsummer Night's Dream* (Act II, Scene i). Once again, imagination must have been required of the audience.

Costumes were the one aspect of stage production in which

trouble and expense were hardly ever spared to obtain a magnificent effect. Only occasionally did they attempt any historical accuracy (almost all Elizabethan productions were what we should call 'modern-dress' ones), but they were appropriate to the characters who wore them: kings were seen to be kings and beggars were similarly unmistakable. It is an odd fact that there was usually no attempt at illusion in the costuming: if a costume looked fine and rich it probably was. Indeed, some of the costumes were almost unbelievably expensive. Henslowe lent his company £19 to buy a cloak, and the Alleyn brothers, well-known actors, gave £20 for a 'black velvet cloak, with sleeves embroidered all with silver and gold, lined with black satin striped with gold'.

With the one exception of the costumes, the 'machinery' of the playhouse was economical and uncomplicated rather than crude and rough, as we can see from this second and more leisurely look at it. This meant that playwrights were stimulated to produce the imaginative effects that they wanted from the language that they used. In the case of a really great writer like Shakespeare, when he had learned his trade in the theatre as an actor, it seems that he received quite enough assistance of a mechanical and structural kind without having irksome restrictions and conventions imposed on him; it is interesting to try to guess what he would have done with the highly complex apparatus of a modern television studio. We can see when we look back to his time that he used his instrument, the Elizabethan theatre, to the full, but placed his ultimate reliance on the communication between his imagination and that of his audience through the medium of words. It is, above all, his rich and wonderful use of language that must have made play-going at that time a memorable experience for people of widely different kinds. Fortunately, the deep satisfaction of appreciating and enjoying Shakespeare's work can be ours also, if we are willing to overcome the language difficulty produced by the passing of time.

Shakespeare: A Timeline

Very little indeed is known about Shakespeare's private life; the facts included here are almost the only indisputable ones. The dates of Shakespeare's plays are those on which they were first produced.

1558   Queen Elizabeth crowned.

1561   Francis Bacon born.

1564   Christopher Marlowe born.   William Shakespeare born, April 23rd, baptized April 26th.

1566   Shakespeare's brother, Gilbert, born.

1567   Mary, Queen of Scots, deposed.
James VI (later James I of England) crowned King of Scotland.

1572   Ben Jonson born.
Lord Leicester's Company (of players) licensed; later called Lord Strange's, then the Lord Chamberlain's and finally (under James) the King's Men.

1573   John Donne born.

1574   The Common Council of London directs that all plays and playhouses in London must be licensed.

1576   James Burbage builds the first public playhouse, The Theatre, at Shoreditch, outside the walls of the City.

1577   Francis Drake begins his voyage round the world (completed 1580).
Holinshed's Chronicles of England, Scotland and Ireland published (which

Shakespeare later used extensively).

1582		Shakespeare married to Anne Hathaway.
1583	The Queen's Company founded by royal warrant.	Shakespeare's daughter, Susanna, born.
1585		Shakespeare's twins, Hamnet and Judith, born.
1586	Sir Philip Sidney, the Elizabethan ideal 'Christian knight', poet, patron, soldier, killed at Zutphen in the Low Countries.	
1587	Mary, Queen of Scots, beheaded. Marlowe's *Tamburlaine (Part I)* first staged.	
1588	Defeat of the Spanish Armada. Marlowe's *Tamburlaine (Part II)* first staged.	
1589	Marlowe's *Jew of Malta* and Kyd's *Spanish Tragedy* (a 'revenge tragedy' and one of the most popular plays of Elizabethan times).	
1590	Spenser's *Faerie Queene* (Books I–III) published.	
1592	Marlowe's *Doctor Faustus* and *Edward II* first staged. Witchcraft trials in Scotland. Robert Greene, a rival playwright, refers to Shakespeare as 'an upstart crow' and 'the only Shake-scene in a country'.	*Titus Andronicus* *Henry VI, Parts I, II and III* *Richard III*
1593	London theatres closed by the plague. Christopher Marlowe killed in a Deptford tavern.	*Two Gentlemen of Verona* *Comedy of Errors* *The Taming of the Shrew* *Love's Labour's Lost*
1594	Shakespeare's company becomes The Lord Chamberlain's Men.	*Romeo and Juliet*

1595	Raleigh's first expedition to Guiana. Last expedition of Drake and Hawkins (both died).	*Richard II* *A Midsummer Night's Dream*
1596	Spenser's *Faerie Queene* (Books IV–VI) published. James Burbage buys rooms at Blackfriars and begins to convert them into a theatre.	*King John* *The Merchant of Venice* Shakespeare's son Hamnet dies. Shakespeare's father is granted a coat of arms.
1597	James Burbage dies, his son Richard, a famous actor, turns the Blackfriars Theatre into a private playhouse.	*Henry IV (Part I)* Shakespeare buys and redecorates New Place at Stratford.
1598	Death of Philip II of Spain	*Henry IV (Part II)* *Much Ado About Nothing*
1599	Death of Edmund Spenser. The Globe Theatre completed at Bankside by Richard and Cuthbert Burbage.	*Henry V* *Julius Caesar* *As You Like It*
1600	Fortune Theatre built at Cripplegate. East India Company founded for the extension of English trade and influence in the East. The Children of the Chapel begin to use the hall at Blackfriars.	*Merry Wives of Windsor* *Troilus and Cressida*
1601		*Hamlet*
1602	Sir Thomas Bodley's library opened at Oxford.	*Twelfth Night*
1603	Death of Queen Elizabeth. James I comes to the throne. Shakespeare's company becomes The King's Men. Raleigh tried, condemned and sent to the Tower	
1604	Treaty of peace with Spain	*Measure for Measure* *Othello* *All's Well that Ends Well*
1605	The Gunpowder Plot: an attempt by a group of Catholics to blow up the Houses of Parliament.	

1606	Guy Fawkes and other plotters executed.	*Macbeth* *King Lear*
1607	Virginia, in America, colonized. A great frost in England.	*Antony and Cleopatra* *Timon of Athens* *Coriolanus* Shakespeare's daughter, Susanna, married to Dr. John Hall.
1608	The company of the Children of the Chapel Royal (who had performed at Blackfriars for ten years) is disbanded. John Milton born. Notorious pirates executed in London.	Richard Burbage leases the Blackfriars Theatre to six of his fellow actors, including Shakespeare. Pericles, Prince of Tyre
1609		Shakespeare's Sonnets published.
1610	A great drought in England	*Cymbeline*
1611	Chapman completes his great translation of the *Iliad*, the story of Troy. Authorized Version of the Bible published.	*A Winter's Tale* *The Tempest*
1612	Webster's *The White Devil* first staged.	Shakespeare's brother, Gilbert, dies.
1613	Globe theatre burnt down during a performance of *Henry VIII* (the firing of small cannon set fire to the thatched roof). Webster's *Duchess of Malfi* first staged.	*Henry VIII* *Two Noble Kinsmen* Shakespeare buys a house at Blackfriars.
1614	Globe Theatre rebuilt in 'far finer manner than before'.	
1616	Ben Jonson publishes his plays in one volume. Raleigh released from the Tower in order to prepare an expedition to the gold mines of Guiana.	Shakespeare's daughter, Judith, marries Thomas Quiney. Death of Shakespeare on his birthday, April 23rd.
1618	Raleigh returns to England and is executed on the charge for which he was imprisoned in 1603.	
1623	Publication of the Folio edition of Shakespeare's plays	Death of Anne Shakespeare (née Hathaway).

Life & Times

William Shakespeare the Playwright

There exists a curious paradox when it comes to the life of William Shakespeare. He easily has more words written about him than any other famous English writer, yet we know the least about him. This inevitably means that most of what is written about him is either fabrication or speculation. The reason why so little is known about Shakespeare is that he wasn't a novelist or a historian or a man of letters. He was a playwright, and playwrights were considered fairly low on the social pecking order in Elizabethan society. Writing plays was about providing entertainment for the masses – the great unwashed. It was the equivalent to being a journalist for a tabloid newspaper.

In fact, we only know of Shakespeare's work because two of his friends had the foresight to collect his plays together following his death and have them printed. The only reason they did so was apparently because they rated his talent and thought it would be a shame if his words were lost.

Consequently his body of work has ever since been assessed and reassessed as the greatest contribution to English literature. That is despite the fact that we know that different printers took it upon themselves to heavily edit the material they worked from. We also know that Elizabethan plays were worked and reworked frequently, so that they evolved over time until they were honed to perfection, which means that many different hands played their part in the active writing process. It would therefore be fair to say that any play attributed to Shakespeare is unlikely to contain a great deal of original input. Even the plots were based on well known historical events, so it would be hard to know what fragments of any Shakespeare play came from that single mind.

One might draw a comparison with the Christian bible, which remains such a compelling read because it came from the collaboration of many contributors and translators over centuries, who each adjusted the stories until they could no longer be improved. As virtually nothing is known of Shakespeare's life and even less about his method of working, we shall never know the truth about his plays. They certainly contain some very elegant phrasing, clever plot devices and plenty of words never before seen in print, but as to whether Shakespeare invented them from a unique imagination or whether he simply took them from others around him is anyone's guess.

The best bet seems to be that Shakespeare probably took the lead role in devising the original drafts of the plays, but was open to collaboration from any source when it came to developing them into workable scripts for effective performances. He would have had to work closely with his fellow actors in rehearsals, thereby finding out where to edit, abridge, alter, reword and so on.

In turn, similar adjustments would have occurred in his absence, so that definitive versions of his plays never really existed. In effect Shakespeare was only responsible for providing the framework of plays, upon which others took liberties over time. This wasn't helped by the fact that the English language itself was not definitive at that time either. The consequence was that people took it upon themselves to spell words however they pleased or to completely change words and phrasing to suit their own preferences.

It is easy to see then, that Shakespeare's plays were always going to have lives of their own, mutating and distorting in detail like Chinese whispers. The culture of creative preservation was simply not established in Elizabethan England. Creative ownership of Shakespeare's plays was lost to him as soon as he released them into the consciousness of others. They saw nothing wrong with taking his ideas and running with them, because no one had ever suggested that one shouldn't, and Shakespeare probably regarded his work in the same way. His plays weren't sacrosanct works of art, they were templates for theatre folk to make their livings from, so they had every right to mould them into productions that drew in the crowds as effectively as possible. Shakespeare was like the helmsman of a sailing ship, steering the vessel but wholly reliant on the team work of his crew to arrive at the desired destination.

It seems that Shakespeare certainly had a natural gift, but the genius of his plays may be attributable to the collective efforts of Shakespeare and others. It is a rather satisfying notion to think that *his* plays might actually be the creative outpourings of the Elizabethan milieu in which Shakespeare immersed himself. That makes them important social documents as well as seminal works of the English language.

Money in Shakespeare's Day

It is extremely difficult, if not impossible, to relate the value of money in our time to its value in another age and to compare prices of commodities today and in the past. Many items *are* simply not comparable on grounds of quality or serviceability.

There was a bewildering variety of coins in use in Elizabethan England. As nearly all English and European coins were gold or silver, they had intrinsic value apart from their official value. This meant that foreign coins circulated freely in England and were officially recognized, for example the French crown (écu) worth about 30p (72 cents), and the Spanish ducat worth about 33p (79 cents). The following table shows some of the coins mentioned by Shakespeare and their relation to one another.

GOLD	British	American	SILVER	British	American
sovereign (heavy type)	£1.50	$3.60	shilling	10p	24c
sovereign (light type)	66p–£l	$1.58–$2.40	groat	1.5p	4c
angel					
royal	33p–50p	79c–$1.20			
noble	50p	$1.20			
crown	25p	60c			

A comparison of the following prices in Shakespeare's time with the prices of the same items today will give some idea of the change in the value of money.

ITEM	PRICE British	American	ITEM	PRICE British	American
beef, per lb.	0.5p	1c	cherries (lb.)	1p	2c
mutton, leg	7.5p	18c	7 oranges	1p	2c
rabbit	3.5p	9c	1 lemon	1p	2c
chicken	3p	8c	cream (quart)	2.5p	6c
potatoes (lb)	10p	24c	sugar (lb.)	£1	$2.40
carrots (bunch)	1p	2c	sack (wine) (gallon)	14p	34c
8 artichokes	4p	9c	tobacco (oz.)	25p	60c
1 cucumber	1p	2c	biscuits (lb.)	12.5p	30c

INTRODUCTION

Hamlet seems always to have been the most discussed work of literature in the world. The range of possible responses runs from Tolstoy's famously perverse dismissal of the play as unintelligible (Tolstoy, 1937), to the most far-reaching claims for its insight into the Nature of the Cosmos. Understanding of it has been sought from analyses of Hamlet's personality (in our century often in terms of Freudian psychoanalytical theory); of the play's place in a supposed tradition of revenge plays; of Elizabethan pneumatology (the study of ghosts and other spirits); of Shakespeare's biography; and along other routes too numerous even to mention. It has been adapted as play, film, novel, story and cartoon, countless times throughout the world by writers major, minor, and somewhere in between. It has been classed as a tragedy, a 'problem play', a 'revenge play', and seen as entirely *sui generis*. Commentators speak unanimously of its being Shakespeare's most enigmatic work – 'the most problematic play ever written by Shakespeare or any other playwright' (Levin, 1956). Like a black hole, it has tended to assimilate to itself all questions asked of it, so that it seems to anticipate the most bizarre readings and even to sponsor mutually incompatible ones simultaneously. It can be 'insistently incoherent and just as insistently coherent' (Booth, 1969); the audience is drawn into its contradictions, deconstructing and then reconstructing the paradoxes (see Calderwood, 1983). As time has familiarised the play to readers and audiences throughout the world, its performance has become a hallowed ritual – yet this is a work which by Elizabethan standards is remarkable and unconventional, notably in its realism.

In descending to such mundane matters as what happens in the play, readers coming to it for the first time will find themselves pondering many questions.

Interpretation of Acts 1-3 involves issues, for example, concerning the nature of the Ghost (is Hamlet's mission divinely or demonically inspired?); the justice of his view of Claudius; whether or not Claudius sees, or understands, the play in Act 3 Scene 2; and whether Hamlet does or does not mistake Polonius for Claudius in Act 3 Scene 4. Readings of later parts turn on, amongst other things, how far Hamlet's madness is considered to be real and how far feigned; whether Fortinbras is seen as an unruly hot-head or a worthy heir to the throne; and whether the Hamlet of Act 5 is the familiar part-failure of the past or the repository of 'a mysterious and beautiful disinterestedness' (Bloom, 1989). All this is to say nothing of the by now ancient question, 'Why does Hamlet delay in killing Claudius?', a question widely posed, frequently but variously answered, and now coming to seem less than useful.

But it would be wrong to lay the stress exclusively on the 'problems', the 'questions', the 'mystery' of *Hamlet*. Though nothing is more certain than that they will continue to engender debate, the play will be read and watched for other reasons. The 'particular excellence' of *Hamlet* was for Johnson its 'variety', its mingling of merriment and solemnity, frivolity and horror (Johnson, 1765). Something of this is echoed in Tillyard's sense that 'simply as a play of things happening, of one event being bred out of another, and of each event being described with appropriate and unwearied brilliance, *Hamlet* is supreme' (Tillyard, 1950). Superlatives seem to come cheap with this play, but *Hamlet*'s readers will undoubtedly continue to find it 'the world's most sheerly entertaining tragedy, the cleverest, perhaps even the funniest' (Everett, 1989); they will also find Shakespeare's power to entertain uniquely combined in it with his power to mean.

LIST OF CHARACTERS

Claudius	King of Denmark
Hamlet	son to the former and nephew to the present King
Polonius	Lord Chamberlain
Horatio	friend to Hamlet
Laertes	son to Polonius
Voltemand	A Gentleman,
Cornelius	A Gentleman
Rosencrantz, Guildenstern, Osric,	Courtiers
A Priest	
Marcellus, Bernardo	officers
Francisco	a soldier
Reynaldo	servant to Polonius
Players	
Two Clowns grave-diggers	
Fortinbras	Prince of Norway
A Norwegian Captain	
English Ambassadors	
Gertrude	Queen of Denmark, and mother of Hamlet
Ophelia	daughter to Polonius
Ghost of Hamlet's Father	

Lords, Ladies, Officers, Soldiers, Sailors, Messengers, and Attendants.

The Scene: Denmark

ACT ONE

Scene I

Elsinore. The guard-platform of the Castle.

[FRANCISCO *at his post. Enter to him* BERNARDO.]

Bernardo
Who's there?
Francisco
Nay, answer me. Stand and unfold yourself.
Bernardo
Long live the King!
Francisco
Bernardo?
Bernardo   5
He.
Francisco
You come most carefully upon your hour.
Bernardo
'Tis now struck twelve; get thee to bed, Francisco.
Francisco
For this relief much thanks. 'Tis bitter cold,
And I am sick at heart.
Bernardo
Have you had quiet guard?   10
Francisco
                          Not a mouse stirring.
Bernardo
Well, good night.
If you do meet Horatio and Marcellus,
The rivals of my watch, bid them make haste.

[*Enter* HORATIO *and* MARCELLUS.]

Francisco
I think I hear them. Stand, ho! Who is there?
Horatio
Friends to this ground.

Marcellus

15   And liegemen to the Dane.

Francisco

  Give you good night.

Marcellus

                    O, farewell, honest soldier!
  Who hath relie'd you?

Francisco

                  Bernardo hath my place.
  Give you good night.

                    [Exit.]

Marcellus

                    Holla, Bernado!

Bernardo

                              Say –
  What, is Horatio there?

Horatio

                    A piece of him.

Bernardo

20 Welcome, Horatio; welcome, good Marcellus.

Horatio

  What, has this thing appear'd again to-night?

Bernardo

  I have seen nothing.

Marcellus

  Horatio says 'tis but our fantasy,
  And will not let belief take hold of him
25 Touching this dreaded sight, twice seen of us;
  Therefore I have entreated him along
  With us to watch the minutes of this night.
  That, if again this apparition come,
  He may approve our eyes and speak to it.

Horatio

  Tush, tush, 'twill not appear.

Bernardo

30   Sit down awhile.
  And let us once again assail your ears.

That are so fortified against our story,
What we have two nights seen.
Horatio

Well, sit we down,
And let us hear Bernardo speak of this.
Bernardo
Last night of all, 35
When yond same star that's westward from the
pole
Had made his course t'illume that part of heaven
Where now it burns, Marcellus and myself,
The bell then beating one –

[Enter GHOST.]

Marcellus
Peace, break thee off; look where it comes again. 40
Bernardo
In the same figure, like the King that's dead.
Marcellus
Thou art a scholar; speak to it, Horatio.
Bernardo
Looks 'a not like the King? Mark it, Horatio.
Horatio
Most like. It harrows me with fear and wonder.
Bernardo
It would be spoke to. 45
Marcellus

Question it, Horatio.
Horatio
What art thou that usurp'st this time of night
Together with that fair and warlike form
In which the majesty of buried Denmark
Did sometimes march? By heaven I charge thee,
speak!
Marcellus
It is offended.
Bernardo

See, it stalks away. 50

Horatio
Stay! speak, speak! I charge thee, speak!

[Exit GHOST.*]*

Marcellus
'Tis gone, and will not answer.
Bernardo
How now, Horatio! You tremble and look pale.
Is not this something more than fantasy?
55   What think you on't?
Horatio
Before my God, I might not this believe
Without the sensible and true avouch
Of mine own eyes.
Marcellus
               Is it not like the King?
Horatio
As thou art to thyself:
60   Such was the very armour he had on
When he the ambitious Norway combated;
So frown'd he once when, in an angry parle,
He smote the sledded Polacks on the ice.
'Tis strange.
Marcellus
65   Thus twice before, and jump at this dead hour,
With martial stalk hath he gone by our watch.
Horatio
In what particular thought to work I know not;
But, in the gross and scope of mine opinion,
This bodes some strange eruption to our state.
Marcellus
70   Good now, sit down, and tell me, he that knows,
Why this same strict and most observant watch
So nightly toils the subject of the land;
And why such daily cast of brazen cannon,
And foreign mart for implements of war;
Why such impress of shipwrights, whose sore
75   task

Does not divide the Sunday from the week;
What might be toward, that this sweaty haste
Doth make the night joint-labourer with the day:
Who is't that can inform me?

Horatio

                        That can I;
At least, the whisper goes so. Our last king,   80
Whose image even but now appear'd to us,
Was, as you know, by Fortinbras of Norway,
Thereto prick'd on by a most emulate pride,
Dar'd to the combat; in which our valiant
    Hamlet –
For so this side of our known world esteem'd
    him –   85
Did slay this Fortinbras; who, by a seal'd
    compact,
Well ratified by law and heraldry,
Did forfeit, with his life, all those his lands
Which he stood seiz'd of, to the conqueror;
Against the which a moiety competent   90
Was gaged by our king; which had return'd
To the inheritance of Fortinbras,
Had he been vanquisher; as, by the same
    comart
And carriage of the article design'd,
His fell to Hamlet. Now, sir, young Fortinbras,   95
Of unimproved mettle hot and full,
Hath in the skirts of Norway, here and there,
Shark'd up a list of lawless resolutes,
For food and diet, to some enterprise
That hath a stomach in't; which is no other,   100
As it doth well appear unto our state,
But to recover of us, by strong hand
And terms compulsatory, those foresaid lands
So by his father lost; and this, I take it.
Is the main motive of our preparations,   105
The source of this our watch, and the chief
    head

Of this post-haste and romage in the land.
Bernardo
I think it be no other but e'en so,
Well may it sort, that this portentous figure
110   Comes armed through our watch; so like the King
That was and is the question of these wars.
Horatio
A mote it is to trouble the mind's eye.
In the most high and palmy state of Rome.
A little ere the mightiest Julius fell,
115   The graves stood tenantless, and the sheeted dead
Did squeak and gibber in the Roman streets;
As, stars with trains of fire, and dews of blood,
Disasters in the sun; and the moist star
Upon whose influence Neptune's empire stands
120   Was sick almost to doomsday with eclipse,
And even the like precurse of fear'd events,
As harbingers preceding still the fates
And prologue to the omen coming on,
Have heaven and earth together demonstrated
125   Unto our climatures and countrymen.

[Re-enter GHOST.*]*

But, soft, behold! Lo, where it comes again!
I'll cross it, though it blast me. Stay, illusion.

*[*GHOST *spreads its arms.]*

If thou hast any sound or use of voice,
Speak to me.
130   If there be any good thing to be done,
That may to thee do ease and grace to me,
Speak to me.
If thou art privy to thy country's fate,
Which happily foreknowing may avoid,
135   O, speak!
Or if thou hast uphoarded in thy life

Extorted treasure in the womb of earth,
For which, they say, you spirits oft walk in
    death,

[The cock crows.]

Speak of it. Stay, and speak. Stop it, Marcellus.
Marcellus
    Shall I strike at it with my partisan?   140
Horatio
    Do, if it will not stand.
Bernardo
                              'Tis here!
Horatio
                                        'Tis here!
Marcellus
    'Tis gone!   *[Exit* GHOST.*]*
    We do it wrong, being so majestical,
    To offer it the show of violence;
    For it is, as the air, invulnerable,   145
    And our vain blows malicious mockery.
Bernardo
    It was about to speak, when the cock crew.
Horatio
    And then it started like a guilty thing
    Upon a fearful summons. I have heard
    The cock, that is the trumpet to the morn,   150
    Doth with his lofty and shrill-sounding throat
    Awake the god of day; and at his warning,
    Whether in sea or fire, in earth or air,
    Th' extravagant and erring spirit hies
    To his confine; and of the truth herein   155
    This present object made probation.
Marcellus
    It faded on the crowing of the cock.
    Some say that ever 'gainst that season comes
    Wherein our Saviour's birth is celebrated,
    This bird of dawning singeth all night long;   160
    And then, they say, no spirit dare stir abroad.

The nights are wholesome, then no planets strike,
No fairy takes, nor witch hath power to
   charm.
So hallowed and so gracious is that time.

Horatio

165   So have I heard, and do in part believe it.
But look, the morn, in russet mantle clad,
Walks o'er the dew of yon high eastward hill.
Break we our watch up; and, by my advice,
Let us impart what we have seen to-night
170   Unto young Hamlet; for, upon my life,
This spirit, dumb to us, will speak to him.
Do you consent we shall acquaint him with it,
As needful in our loves, fitting our duty?

Marcellus

Let's do't, I pray; and I this morning know
175   Where we shall find him most convenient.

[Exeunt.]

Scene II

Elsinore. The Castle.

[Flourish. Enter CLAUDIUS KING OF DENMARK,
GERTRUDE THE QUEEN, *and* COUNCILLORS, *including*
POLONIUS, *his son* LAERTES, VOLTEMAND,
CORNELIUS, *and* HAMLET.*]*

King

Though yet of Hamlet our dear brother's death
The memory be green; and that it us befitted
To bear our hearts in grief, and our whole
  kingdom
To be contracted in one brow of woe;
Yet so far hath discretion fought with nature   5
That we with wisest sorrow think on him,
Together with remembrance of ourselves.
Therefore our sometime sister, now our queen,
Th' imperial jointress to this warlike state,
Have we, as 'twere with a defeated joy,   10
With an auspicious and a dropping eye,
With mirth in funeral, and with dirge in
  marriage,
In equal scale weighing delight and dole,
Taken to wife; nor have we herein barr'd
Your better wisdoms, which have freely gone   15
With this affair along. For all, our thanks.
Now follows that you know: young Fortinbras,
Holding a weak supposal of our worth,
Or thinking by our late dear brother's death
Our state to be disjoint and out of frame,   20
Co-leagued with this dream of his advantage –
He hath not fail'd to pester us with message
Importing the surrender of those lands
Lost by his father, with all bands of law,
To our most valiant brother. So much for him.   25
Now for ourself, and for this time of meeting,
Thus much the business is: we have here writ

To Norway, uncle of young Fortinbras –
Who, impotent and bed-rid, scarcely hears
30 Of this his nephew's purpose – to suppress
His further gait herein, in that the levies,
The lists, and full proportions, are all made
Out of his subject; and we here dispatch
You, good Cornelius, and you, Voltemand,
35 For bearers of this greeting to old Norway;
Giving to you no further personal power
To business with the King more than the scope
Of these delated articles allow.
Farewell; and let your haste commend your
duty.
Cornelius, Voltemand
40 In that and all things will we show our duty.
King
We doubt it nothing, heartily farewell.

[Exeunt VOLTEMAND *and* CORNELIUS.*]*

And now, Laertes, what's the news with you?
You told us of some suit; what is't, Laertes?
You cannot speak of reason to the Dane
And lose your voice. What wouldst thou beg,
45 Laertes,
That shall not be my offer, not thy asking?
The head is not more native to the heart,
The hand more instrumental to the mouth,
Than is the throne of Denmark to thy father.
What wouldst thou have, Laertes?
Laertes
50   My dread lord,
Your leave and favour to return to France;
From whence though willingly I came to
Denmark
To show my duty in your coronation,
Yet now, I must confess, that duty done,
My thoughts and wishes bend again toward
55 France,

And bow them to your gracious leave and
   pardon.
King
  Have you your gracious father's leave? What
    says Polonius?
Polonius
  'A hath, my lord, wrung from me my slow
    leave
  By laboursome petition; and at last
  Upon his will I seal'd my hard consent.   60
  I do beseech you, give him leave to go.
King
  Take thy fair hour, Laertes: time be thine,
  And thy best graces spend it at thy will!
  But now, my cousin Hamlet, and my son –
Hamlet [Aside]
  A little more than kin, and less than kind.   65
King
  How is it that the clouds still hang on you?
Hamlet
  Not so, my lord; I am too much in the sun.
Queen
  Good Hamlet, cast thy nighted colour off,
  And let thine eye look like a friend on
    Denmark.
  Do not for ever with thy vailed lids   70
  Seek for thy noble father in the dust.
  Thou know'st 'tis common – all that lives must
    die,
  Passing through nature to eternity.
Hamlet
  Ay, madam, it is common.
Queen
                If it be,
  Why seems it so particular with thee?   75
Hamlet
  Seems, madam! Nay, it is; I know not seems.
  'Tis not alone my inky cloak, good mother,

Nor customary suits of solemn black,
Nor windy suspiration of forc'd breath,
80 No, nor the fruitful river in the eye.
Nor the dejected haviour of the visage,
Together with all forms, moods, shapes of grief,
That can denote me truly. These, indeed, seem;
For they are actions that a man might play;
85 But I have that within which passes show –
These but the trappings and the suits of woe.
 King
'Tis sweet and commendable in your nature,
  Hamlet,
To give these mourning duties to your father;
But you must know your father lost a father;
90 That father lost his; and the survivor bound,
In filial obligation, for some term
To do obsequious sorrow. But to persever
In obstinate condolement is a course
Of impious stubbornness; 'tis unmanly grief;
95 It shows a will most incorrect to heaven,
A heart unfortified, a mind impatient,
An understanding simple and unschool'd;
For what we know must be, and is as common
As any the most vulgar thing to sense,
100 Why should we in our peevish opposition
Take it to heart? Fie! 'tis a fault to heaven,
A fault against the dead, a fault to nature,
To reason most absurd; whose common theme;
Is death of fathers, and who still hath cried,
105 From the first corse till he that died to-day,
'This must be so'. We pray you throw to earth
This unprevailing woe, and think of us
As of a father; for let the world take note
You are the most immediate to our throne:
110 And with no less nobility of love
Than that which dearest father bears his son
Do I impart toward you. For your intent
In going back to school in Wittenberg,

It is most retrograde to our desire;
And we beseech you bend you to remain   115
Here, in the cheer and comfort of our eye,
Our chiefest courtier, cousin, and our son.

Queen

Let not thy mother lose her prayers, Hamlet:
I pray thee stay with us; go not to Wittenberg.

Hamlet

I shall in all my best obey you, madam.   120

King

Why, 'tis a loving and a fair reply.
Be as ourself in Denmark. Madam, come:
This gentle and unforc'd accord of Hamlet
Sits smiling to my heart; in grace whereof,
No jocund health that Denmark drinks to-day   125
But the great cannon to the clouds shall tell,
And the King's rouse the heaven shall bruit
    again,
Re-speaking earthly thunder. Come away.

[Flourish. Exeunt all but HAMLET.*]*

Hamlet

O, that this too too solid flesh would melt,
Thaw, and resolve itself into a dew!   130
Or that the Everlasting had not fix'd
His canon 'gainst self-slaughter! O God! God!
How weary, stale, flat, and unprofitable,
Seem to me all the uses of this world!
Fie on't! Ah, fie! 'tis an unweeded garden,   135
That grows to seed; things rank and gross in
    nature
Possess it merely. That it should come to this!
But two months dead! Nay, not so much, not
    two.
So excellent a king that was to this
Hyperion to a satyr; so loving to my mother.   140
That he might not beteem the winds of heaven
Visit her face too roughly. Heaven and earth!

Must I remember? Why, she would hang on
   him
As if increase of appetite had grown
145 By what it fed on; and yet, within a month –
Let me not think on't. Frailty, thy name is
   woman! –
A little month, or ere those shoes were old
With which she followed my poor father's
   body,
Like Niobe, all tears – why she, even she –
150 O God! a beast that wants discourse of reason
Would have mourn'd longer – married with my
   uncle,
My father's brother; but no more like my father
Than I to Hercules. Within a month,
Ere yet the salt of most unrighteous tears
155 Had left the flushing in her galled eyes,
She married. O, most wicked speed, to post
With such dexterity to incestuous sheets!
It is not, nor it cannot come to good.
But break, my heart, for I must hold my
   tongue.

[Enter HORATIO, MARCELLUS, *and* BERNARDO.*]*

Horatio
Hail to your lordship!
Hamlet
160   I am glad to see you well.
Horatio – or I do forget myself.
Horatio
The same, my lord, and your poor servant ever.
Hamlet
Sir, my good friend. I'll change that name with
   you.
And what make you from Wittenberg, Horatio?
165 Marcellus?
Marcellus
My good lord!

Hamlet

    I am very glad to see you. *[To* BERNARDO*]* Good
      even, sir. –
    But what, in faith, make you from Wittenberg?

Horatio

    A truant disposition, good my lord.

Hamlet

    I would not hear your enemy say so;   170
    Nor shall you do my ear that violence,
    To make it truster of your own report
    Against yourself. I know you are no truant.
    But what is your affair in Elsinore?
    We'll teach you to drink deep ere you depart.   175

Horatio

    My lord, I came to see your father's funeral.

Hamlet

    I prithee do not mock me, fellow student;
    I think it was to see my mother's wedding.

Horatio

    Indeed, my lord, it followed hard upon.

Hamlet

    Thrift, thrift, Horatio! The funeral bak'd-meats   180
    Did coldly furnish forth the marriage tables.
    Would I had met my dearest foe in heaven
    Or ever I had seen that day, Horatio!
    My father – methinks I see my father.

Horatio

    Where, my lord?

Hamlet

                In my mind's eye, Horatio.   185

Horatio

    I saw him once; 'a was a goodly king.

Hamlet

    'A was a man, take him for all in all,
    I shall not look upon his like again.

Horatio

    My lord, I think I saw him yester-night.

Hamlet
190   Saw who?
Horatio
   My lord, the King your father.
Hamlet
                              The King my father!
Horatio
   Season your admiration for a while
   With an attent ear, till I may deliver,
   Upon the witness of these gentlemen,
   This marvel to you.
Hamlet
195   For God's love, let me hear.
Horatio
   Two nights together had these gentlemen,
   Marcellus and Bernardo, on their watch,
   In the dead waste and middle of the night,
   Been thus encount'red. A figure like your father,
200   Armed at point exactly, cap-a-pe,
   Appears before them, and with solemn march
   Goes slow and stately by them; thrice he walk'd
   By their oppress'd and fear-surprised eyes,
   Within his truncheon's length; whilst they,
      distill'd
205   Almost to jelly with the act of fear,
   Stand dumb and speak not to him. This to me
   In dreadful secrecy impart they did;
   And I with them the third night kept the
      watch;
   Where, as they had delivered, both in time,
   Form of the thing, each word made true and
210   good,
   The apparition comes. I knew your father;
   These hands are not more like.
Hamlet
                              But where was this?
Marcellus
   My lord, upon the platform where we watch.

Hamlet
Did you not speak to it?
Horatio

My lord, I did;
But answer made it none; yet once methought   215
It lifted up it head and did address
Itself to motion, like as it would speak;
But even then the morning cock crew loud,
And at the sound it shrunk in haste away
And vanish'd from our sight.
Hamlet

'Tis very strange.   220

Horatio
As I do live, my honour'd lord, 'tis true;
And we did think it writ down in our duty
To let you know of it.
Hamlet
Indeed, indeed, sirs, but this troubles me.
Hold you the watch to-night?
All

We do, my lord.   225

Hamlet
Arm'd, say you?
All

Arm'd, my lord.

Hamlet
From top to toe?
All

My lord, from head to foot.

Hamlet
Then saw you not his face?
Horatio
O yes, my lord; he wore his beaver up.
Hamlet
What, look'd he frowningly?   230
Horatio
A countenance more in sorrow than in anger.

Hamlet
  Pale or red?
Horatio
  Nay, very pale.
Hamlet
                And fix'd his eyes upon you?
Horatio
  Most constantly.
Hamlet
                I would I had been there.
Horatio
235   It would have much amaz'd you.
Hamlet
  Very like, very like. Stay'd it long?
Horatio
  While one with moderate haste might tell a
     hundred.
Both
  Longer, longer.
Horatio
  Not when I saw't.
Hamlet
  His beard was grizzl'd – no?
Horatio
240   It was, as I have seen it in his life, A sable
     silver'd.
Hamlet
                I will watch to-night;
  Perchance 'twill walk again.
Horatio
                        I warr'nt it will.
Hamlet
  If it assume my noble father's person,
  I'll speak to it, though hell itself should gape
245   And bid me hold my peace. I pray you all,
  If you have hitherto conceal'd this sight,
  Let it be tenable in your silence still;
  And whatsomever else shall hap to-night,

Give it an understanding, but no tongue;
I will requite your loves. So, fare you well – 250
Upon the platform, 'twixt eleven and twelve,
I'll visit you.

All

                Our duty to your honour.

Hamlet

Your loves, as mine to you; farewell.

         [Exeunt all but HAMLET.*]*

My father's spirit in arms! All is not well.
I doubt some foul play. Would the night were
    come! 255
Till then sit still, my soul. Foul deeds will rise,
Though all the earth o'erwhelm them, to men's
    eyes.

           [Exit.]

Scene III

Elsinore. The house of Polonius.

[Enter LAERTES and OPHELIA his sister.]

Laertes
My necessaries are embark'd. Farewell. And,
    sister, as the winds give benefit
And convoy is assistant, do not sleep,
But let me hear from you.

Ophelia
                    Do you doubt that?

Laertes
5   For Hamlet, and the trifling of his favour,
Hold it a fashion and a toy in blood,
A violet in the youth of primy nature,
Forward not permanent, sweet not lasting,
The perfume and suppliance of a minute;
No more.

Ophelia
          No more but so?

Laertes
10   Think it no more;
For nature crescent does not grow alone
In thews and bulk, but as this temple waxes,
The inward service of the mind and soul
Grows wide withal. Perhaps he loves you now,
15   And now no soil nor cautel doth besmirch
The virtue of his will; but you must fear,
His greatness weigh'd, his will is not his own;
For he himself is subject to his birth:
He may not, as unvalued persons do,
20   Carve for himself; for on his choice depends
The sanity and health of this whole state;
And therefore must his choice be circumscrib'd
Unto the voice and yielding of that body
Whereof he is the head. Then if he says he
    loves you,

It fits your wisdom so far to believe it   25
As he in his particular act and place
May give his saying deed; which is no further
Than the main voice of Denmark goes withal.
Then weigh what loss your honour may sustain,
If with too credent ear you list his songs,   30
Or lose your heart, or your chaste treasure open
To his unmast'red importunity.
Fear it, Ophelia, fear it, my dear sister;
And keep you in the rear of your affection,
Out of the shot and danger of desire.   35
The chariest maid is prodigal enough
If she unmask her beauty to the moon.
Virtue itself scapes not calumnious strokes;
The canker galls the infants of the spring
Too oft before their buttons be disclos'd;   40
And in the morn and liquid dew of youth
Contagious blastments are most imminent.
Be wary, then; best safety lies in fear:
Youth to itself rebels, though none else near.

Ophelia

I shall the effect of this good lesson keep   45
As watchman to my heart. But, good my
    brother,
Do not, as some ungracious pastors do.
Show me the steep and thorny way to heaven,
Whiles, like a puff'd and reckless libertine.
Himself the primrose path of dalliance treads   50
And recks not his own rede.

Laertes

                        O, fear me not!

[Enter POLONIUS.*]*

I stay too long. But here my father comes.
A double blessing is a double grace;
Occasion smiles upon a second leave.

Polonius

Yet here, Laertes! Aboard, aboard, for shame!   55

The wind sits in the shoulder of your sail,
And you are stay'd for. There – my blessing
   with thee!
And these few precepts in thy memory
Look thou character. Give thy thoughts no
   tongue,
60   Nor any unproportion'd thought his act.
Be thou familiar, but by no means vulgar.
Those friends thou hast, and their adoption
   tried,
Grapple them to thy soul with hoops of steel;
But do not dull thy palm with entertainment
65   Of each new-hatch'd, unfledg'd courage. Beware
Of entrance to a quarrel; but, being in,
Bear't that th' opposed may beware of thee.
Give every man thy ear, but few thy voice;
Take each man's censure, but reserve thy
   judgment.
70   Costly thy habit as thy purse can buy,
But not express'd in fancy; rich, not gaudy;
For the apparel oft proclaims the man;
And they in France of the best rank and station
Are of a most select and generous choice in
   that.
75   Neither a borrower nor a lender be;
For loan oft loses both itself and friend,
And borrowing dulls the edge of husbandry.
This above all – to thine own self be true,
And it must follow, as the night the day,
80   Thou canst not then be false to any man.
Farewell; my blessing season this in thee!

Laertes

Most humbly do I take my leave, my lord.

Polonius

The time invites you; go, your servants tend.

Laertes

Farewell, Ophelia; and remember well
What I have said to you.

Ophelia

                      'Tis in my memory lock'd,   85
And you yourself shall keep the key of it.

Laertes

Farewell.

[Exit.]

Polonius

What is't. Ophelia, he hath said to you?

Ophelia

So please you, something touching the Lord
Hamlet.

Polonius

Marry, well bethought!   90
'Tis told me he hath very oft of late
Given private time to you; and you yourself
Have of your audience been most free and
    bounteous.
If it be so – as so 'tis put on me,
And that in way of caution – I must tell you   95
You do not understand yourself so clearly
As it behoves my daughter and your honour.
What is between you? Give me up the truth.

Ophelia

He hath, my lord, of late made many tenders
Of his affection to me.   100

Polonius

Affection! Pooh! You speak like a green girl,
Unsifted in such perilous circumstance.
Do you believe his tenders, as you call them?

Ophelia

I do not know, my lord, what I should think.

Polonius

Marry, I will teach you: think yourself a baby   105
That you have ta'en these tenders for true pay
Which are not sterling. Tender yourself more
    dearly;

Or – not to crack the wind of the poor phrase,
Running it thus – you'll tender me a fool.

Ophelia

100   My lord, he hath importun'd me with love
In honourable fashion.

Polonius

Ay, fashion you may call it; go to, go to.

Ophelia

And hath given countenance to his speech, my
    lord,
With almost all the holy vows of heaven.

Polonius

115   Ay, springes to catch woodcocks! I do know,
When the blood burns, how prodigal the soul
Lends the tongue vows. These blazes, daughter,
Giving more light than heat – extinct in both,
Even in their promise, as it is a-making –

120   You must not take for fire. From this time
Be something scanter of your maiden presence;
Set your entreatments at a higher rate
Than a command to parle. For Lord Hamlet,
Believe so much in him, that he is young,

125   And with a larger tether may he walk
Than may be given you. In few, Ophelia,
Do not believe his vows; for they are brokers,
Not of that dye which their investments show,
But mere implorators of unholy suits,

130   Breathing like sanctified and pious bonds,
The better to beguile. This is for all –
I would not, in plain terms, from this time
    forth
Have you so slander any moment leisure
As to give words or talk with the Lord Hamlet.

135   Look to't, I charge you. Come your ways.

Ophelia

I shall obey, my lord.

[Exeunt.]

Scene IV

Elsinore. The guard-platform of the Castle.

[*Enter* HAMLET, HORATIO, *and* MARCELLUS.]

Hamlet
The air bites shrewdly; it is very cold.
Horatio
It is a nipping and an eager air.
Hamlet
What hour now?
Horatio
                I think it lacks of twelve.
Marcellus
No, it is struck.
Horatio
Indeed? I heard it not. It then draws near the
  season   5
Wherein the spirit held his wont to walk.

[*A flourish of trumpets, and two pieces go off.*]

What does this mean, my lord?
Hamlet
The King doth wake to-night and takes his rouse,
Keeps wassail, and the swagg'ring up-spring reels,
And, as he drains his draughts of Rhenish down, 10
The kettle-drum and trumpet thus bray out
The triumph of his pledge.
Horatio
                Is it a custom?
Hamlet
Ay, marry, is't;
But to my mind, though I am native here
And to the manner born, it is a custom   15
More honour'd in the breach than the
  observance.
This heavy-headed revel east and west
Makes us traduc'd and tax'd of other nations;

They clepe us drunkards, and with swinish
    phrase
20   Soil our addition; and, indeed, it takes
From our achievements, though perform'd at
    height,
The pith and marrow of our attribute.
So, oft it chances in particular men
That, for some vicious mole of nature in them,
25   As in their birth, wherein they are not guilty,
Since nature cannot choose his origin;
By the o'ergrowth of some complexion,
Oft breaking down the pales and forts of
    reason;
Or by some habit that too much o'er-leavens
30   The form of plausive manners – that these
    men.
Carrying, I say, the stamp of one defect,
Being nature's livery or fortune's star,
His virtues else, be they as pure as grace,
As infinite as man may undergo,
35   Shall in the general censure take corruption
From that particular fault. The dram of eale
Doth all the noble substance of a doubt
To his own scandal.

[Enter GHOST.*]*

Horatio
                    Look, my lord, it comes.
Hamlet
Angels and ministers of grace defend us!
40   Be thou a spirit of health or goblin damn'd,
Bring with thee airs from heaven or blasts from
    hell,
Be thy intents wicked or charitable,
Thou com'st in such a questionable shape
That I will speak to thee. I'll call thee Hamlet,
45   King, father, royal Dane. O, answer me!
Let me not burst in ignorance, but tell

Why thy canoniz'd bones, hearsed in death,
Have burst their cerements; why the sepulchre
Wherein we saw thee quietly enurn'd
Hath op'd his ponderous and marble jaws   50
To cast thee up again. What may this mean
That thou, dead corse, again in complete steel
Revisits thus the glimpses of the moon,
Making night hideous, and we fools of nature
So horridly to shake our disposition   55
With thoughts beyond the reaches of our
    souls?
Say, why is this? wherefore? What should we
    do?

[GHOST beckons HAMLET.]

Horatio
It beckons you to go away with it,
As if it some impartment did desire
To you alone.
Marcellus
                Look with what courteous action   60
It waves you to a more removed ground.
But do not go with it.
Horatio
                        No, by no means.
Hamlet
It will not speak; then I will follow it.
Horatio
Do not, my lord.
Hamlet
                Why, what should be the fear?
I do not set my life at a pin's fee;   65
And for my soul, what can it do to that,
Being a thing immortal as itself?
It waves me forth again; I'll follow it.
Horatio
What if it tempt you toward the flood, my
    lord,

70   Or to the dreadful summit of the cliff
That beetles o'er his base into the sea,
And there assume some other horrible form,
Which might deprive your sovereignty of reason
And draw you into madness? Think of it:
75   The very place puts toys of desperation,
Without more motive, into every brain
That looks so many fathoms to the sea
And hears it roar beneath.

Hamlet
                                 It waves me still.
Go on; I'll follow thee.

Marcellus
You shall not go, my lord.

Hamlet
80   Hold off your hands.

Horatio
Be rul'd; you shall not go.

Hamlet
                         My fate cries out,
And makes each petty arture in this body
As hardy as the Nemean lion's nerve.

*[*GHOST *beckons.]*

Still am I call'd. Unhand me, gentlemen.
By heaven, I'll make a ghost of him that lets
85   me.
I say, away! Go on; I'll follow thee.

[Exeunt GHOST *and* HAMLET.*]*

Horatio
He waxes desperate with imagination.

Marcellus
Let's follow; 'tis not fit thus to obey him.

Horatio
Have after. To what issue will this come?

Marcellus
90   Something is rotten in the state of Denmark.

Horatio
    Heaven will direct it.
Marcellus
                              Nay, let's follow him.

                [Exeunt.]

Scene V

Elsinore. The battlements of the Castle.

[*Enter* GHOST *and* HAMLET.]

Hamlet
Whither wilt thou lead me? Speak. I'll go no
further.

Ghost
Mark me.

Hamlet
       I will.

Ghost
          My hour is almost come,
When I to sulph'rous and tormenting flames
Must render up myself.

Hamlet
          Alas, poor ghost!

Ghost
5   Pity me not, but lend thy serious hearing
To what I shall unfold.

Hamlet
          Speak; I am bound to hear.

Ghost
So art thou to revenge, when thou shalt hear.

Hamlet
What?

Ghost
I am thy father's spirit,
10   Doom'd for a certain term to walk the night,
And for the day confin'd to fast in fires,
Till the foul crimes done in my days of nature
Are burnt and purg'd away. But that I am
forbid
To tell the secrets of my prison-house,
15   I could a tale unfold whose lightest word
Would harrow up thy soul, freeze thy young
blood,

Make thy two eyes, like stars, start from their
   spheres,
Thy knotted and combined locks to part,
And each particular hair to stand an end,
Like quills upon the fretful porpentine.   20
But this eternal blazon must not be
To ears of flesh and blood. List, list, O, list!
If thou didst ever thy dear father love –

Hamlet

O God!

Ghost

Revenge his foul and most unnatural murder.   25

Hamlet

Murder!

Ghost

Murder most foul, as in the best it is;
But this most foul, strange, and unnatural

Hamlet

Haste me to know't, that I, with wings as swift
As meditation or the thoughts of love,   30
May sweep to my revenge.

Ghost

                   I find thee apt;
And duller shouldst thou be than the fat weed
That roots itself in ease on Lethe wharf,
Wouldst thou not stir in this. Now, Hamlet, hear:
'Tis given out that, sleeping in my orchard,   35
A serpent stung me; so the whole ear of Denmark
Is by a forged process of my death
Rankly abus'd; but know, thou noble youth,
The serpent that did string thy father's life
Now wears his crown.

Hamlet

             O my prophetic soul!   40
My uncle!

Ghost

Ay, that incestuous, that adulterate beast,
With withcraft of his wits, with traitorous gifts –

O wicked wit and gifts that have the power
45 So to seduce! – won to his shameful lust
The will of my most seeming virtuous queen.
O Hamlet, what a falling off was there,
From me, whose love was of that dignity
That it went hand in hand even with the vow
50 I made to her in marriage; and to decline
Upon a wretch whose natural gifts were poor
To those of mine!
But virtue, as it never will be moved,
Though lewdness court it in a shape of heaven,
55 So lust, though to a radiant angel link'd,
Will sate itself in a celestial bed
And prey on garbage.
But soft! methinks I scent the morning air.
Brief let me be. Sleeping within my orchard,
60 My custom always of the afternoon,
Upon my secure hour thy uncle stole,
With juice of cursed hebona in a vial,
And in the porches of my ears did pour
The leperous distilment; whose effect
65 Holds such an enmity with blood of man
That swift as quicksilver it courses through
The natural gates and alleys of the body;
And with a sudden vigour it doth posset
And curd, like eager droppings into milk,
70 The thin and wholesome blood. So did it mine;
And a most instant tetter bark'd about,
Most lazar-like, with vile and loathsome crust,
All my smooth body.
Thus was I, sleeping, by a brother's hand
75 Of life, of crown, of queen, at once dispatch'd;
Cut off even in the blossoms of my sin,
Unhous'led, disappointed, unanel'd;
No reck'ning made, but sent to my account
With all my imperfections on my head.
80 O, horrible! O, horrible! most horrible!
If thou hast nature in thee, bear it not;

Let not the royal bed of Denmark be
A couch for luxury and damned incest.
But, howsomever thou pursuest this act,
Taint not thy mind, nor let thy soul contrive   85
Against thy mother aught; leave her to heaven,
And to those thorns that in her bosom lodge
To prick and sting her. Fare thee well at once.
The glowworm shows the matin to be near,
And gins to pale his uneffectual fire.
Adieu, adieu, adieu! Remember me.   90

                    [Exit]

Hamlet
O all you host of heaven! O earth! What else?
And shall I couple hell? O, fie! Hold, hold, my
    heart;
And you, my sinews, grow not instant old,
But bear me stiffly up. Remember thee!   95
Ay, thou poor ghost, whiles memory holds a
    seat
In this distracted globe. Remember thee!
Yea, from the table of my memory
I'll wipe away all trivial fond records,
All saws of books, all forms, all pressures past, 100
That youth and observation copied there,
And thy commandment all alone shall live
Within the book and volume of my brain,
Unmix'd with baser matter. Yes, by heaven!
O most pernicious woman!   105
O villain, villain, smiling, damned villain!
My tables – meet it is I set it down
That one may smile, and smile, and be a villain;
At least I am sure it may be so in Denmark.

                    [Writing.]

So, uncle, there you are. Now to my word: 110
It is 'Adieu, adieu! Remember me'.
I have sworn't.

                                                    37

Horatio [Within]
   My lord, my lord!

   [Enter HORATIO *and* MARCELLUS.*]*

Marcellus
   Lord Hamlet!
Horatio
   Heavens secure him!
Hamlet
   So be it!
Marcellus
115   Illo, ho, ho, my lord!
Hamlet
   Hillo, ho, ho, boy! Come, bird, come.
Marcellus
   How is't, my noble lord?
Horatio
                        What news, my lord?
Hamlet
   O, wonderful!
Horatio
   Good my lord, tell it.
Hamlet
                     No; you will reveal it.
Horatio
   Not I, my lord, by heaven!
Marcellus
120   Nor I, my lord.
Hamlet
   How say you, then; would heart of man once
      think it?
   But you'll be secret?
Both
                        Ay, by heaven, my lord!
Hamlet
   There's never a villain dwelling in all Denmark
   But he's an arrant knave.

Horatio
    There needs no ghost, my lord, come from the
        grave   125
    To tell us this.
Hamlet
    Why, right; you are in the right;
    And so, without more circumstance at all,
    I hold it fit that we shake hands and part;
    You, as your business and desire shall point you – 130
    For every man hath business and desire,
    Such as it is; and for my own poor part,
    Look you, I will go pray.
Horatio
    These are but wild and whirling words, my
        lord.
Hamlet
    I am sorry they offend you, heartily;
    Yes, faith, heartily.
Horatio
                            There's no offence, my lord.   135
Hamlet
    Yes, by Saint Patrick, but there is, Horatio,
    And much offence too. Touching this vision
        here –
    It is an honest ghost, that let me tell you.
    For your desire to know what is between us,
    O'ermaster't as you may. And now, good friends, 140
    As you are friends, scholars, and soldiers,
    Give me one poor request.
Horatio
                            What is't, my lord? We will.
Hamlet
    Never make known what you have seen
        to-night.
Both
    My lord, we will not.
Hamlet
                            Nay, but swear't.

Horatio
                                        In faith,
My lord, not I.

Marcellus
145   Nor I, my lord, in faith.

Hamlet
Upon my sword.

Marcellus
We have sworn, my lord, already.

Hamlet
Indeed, upon my sword, indeed.

Ghost [Cries under the stage]
Swear.

Hamlet
Ha, ha, boy! say'st thou so? Art thou there,
150   truepenny?
Come on. You hear this fellow in the cellarage:
Consent to swear.

Horatio
                         Propose the oath, my lord.

Hamlet
Never to speak of this that you have seen,
Swear by my sword.

Ghost [Beneath]
155   Swear.

Hamlet
Hic et ubique? Then we'll shift our ground.
Come hither, gentlemen,
And lay your hands again upon my sword.
Swear by my sword
160   Never to speak of this that you have heard.

Ghost [Beneath]
Swear, by his sword.

Hamlet
Well said, old mole! Canst work i' th' earth so
      fast?
A worthy pioneer! Once more remove, good
      friends.

Horatio
O day and night, but this is wondrous strange!
Hamlet
And therefore as a stranger give it welcome.   165
There are more things in heaven and earth,
    Horatio,
Than are dreamt of in your philosophy.
But come.
Here, as before, never, so help you mercy,
How strange or odd some'er I bear myself –   170
As I perchance hereafter shall think meet
To put an antic disposition on –
That you, at such times, seeing me, never shall,
With arms encumb'red thus, or this head-shake,
Or by pronouncing of some doubtful phrase,   175
As 'Well, well, we know' or 'We could, an if we
    would'
Or 'If we list to speak' or 'There be, an if they
    might'
Or such ambiguous giving out, to note
That you know aught of me – this do swear,
So grace and mercy at your most need help
    you.   180
Ghost [Beneath]
Swear.
Hamlet
Rest, rest, perturbed spirit! So, gentlemen,
With all my love I do commend me to you;
And what so poor a man as Hamlet is
May do t'express his love and friending to you, 185
God willing, shall not lack. Let us go in
    together;
And still your fingers on your lips, I pray.
The time is out of joint. O cursed spite,
That ever I was born to set it right!
Nay, come, let's go together.   190

[Exeunt.]

ACT TWO
Scene I

Elsinore. The house of Polonius.

[Enter POLONIUS *and* REYNALDO.*]*

Polonius
Give him this money and these notes,
   Reynaldo.
Reynaldo
I will, my lord.
Polonius
You shall do marvellous wisely, good Reynaldo,
Before you visit him, to make inquire
Of his behaviour.
Reynaldo
5   My lord, I did intend it.
Polonius
Marry, well said; very well said. Look you, sir,
Enquire me first what Danskers are in Paris;
And how, and who, what means, and where
   they keep,
What company, at what expense; and finding
10   By this encompassment and drift of question
That they do know my son, come you more
   nearer
Than your particular demands will touch it.
Take you, as 'twere, some distant knowledge of
   him;
As thus: 'I know his father and his friends,
15   And in part him'. Do you mark this, Reynaldo?
Reynaldo
Ay, very well, my lord.
Polonius
'And in part him – but' you may say 'not well;
But if't be he I mean, he's very wild;

Addicted so and so'; and there put on him
What forgeries you please; marry, none so rank   20
As may dishonour him; take heed of that;
But, sir, such wanton, wild, and usual slips
As are companions noted and most known
To youth and liberty.

Reynaldo

               As gaming, my lord.

Polonius

Ay, or drinking, fencing, swearing, quarrelling,   25
Drabbing – you may go so far.

Reynaldo

My lord, that would dishonour him.

Polonius

Faith, no; as you may season it in the charge.
You must not put another scandal on him,
That he is open to incontinency;   30
That's not my meaning. But breathe his faults
  so quaintly
That they may seem the taints of liberty;
The flash and outbreak of a fiery mind,
A savageness in unreclaimed blood,
Of general assault.

Reynaldo

            But, my good lord –   35

Polonius

Wherefore should you do this?

Reynaldo

             Ay, my lord,
I would know that.

Polonius

          Marry, sir, here's my drift,
And I believe it is a fetch of warrant:
You laying these slight sullies on my son,
As 'twere a thing a little soil'd wi' th' working,   40
Mark you,
Your party in converse, him you would sound,
Having ever seen in the prenominate crimes

The youth you breathe of guilty, be assur'd
45   He closes with you in this consequence –
'Good sir' or so, or 'friend' or 'gentleman'
According to the phrase or the addition
Of man and country.

Reynaldo
                                    Very good, my lord.

Polonius
And then, sir, does 'a this – 'a does –
50   What was I about to say? By the mass,
I was about to say something; where did I leave?

Reynaldo
At 'closes in the consequence', at 'friend or so'
and 'gentleman'.

Polonius
At 'closes in the consequence' – ay, marry,
55   He closes thus: 'I know the gentleman;
I saw him yesterday, or t'other day,
Or then, or then; with such, or such; and, as
        you say,
There was 'a gaming; there o'ertook in's rouse;
There falling out at tennis'; or perchance
60   'I saw him enter such a house of sale'
Videlicet, a brothel, or so forth. See you now
Your bait of falsehood take this carp of truth;
And thus do we of wisdom and of reach,
With windlasses and with assays of bias,
65   By indirections find directions out;
So, by my former lecture and advice,
Shall you my son. You have me, have you not?

Reynaldo
My lord, I have.

Polonius
                                    God buy ye; fare ye well.

Reynaldo
Good my lord!

Polonius
70   Observe his inclination in yourself.

Reynaldo
  I shall, my lord.
Polonius
  And let him ply his music.
Reynaldo

                              Well, my lord.

Polonius
  Farewell!

                    [Exit REYNALDO.*]*

                    [Enter OPHELIA.*]*

            How now, Ophelia! What's the matter?
Ophelia
  O my lord, my lord, I have been so affrighted!
Polonius
  With what, i' th' name of God?   75
Ophelia
  My lord, as I was sewing in my closet,
  Lord Hamlet, with his doublet all unbrac'd,
  No hat upon his head, his stockings fouled,
  Ungart'red and down-gyved to his ankle;
  Pale as his shirt, his knees knocking each other,   80
  And with a look so piteous in purport
  As if he had been loosed out of hell
  To speak of horrors – he comes before me.
Polonius
  Mad for thy love?
Ophelia

                  My lord, I do not know,
  But truly I do fear it.
Polonius

                  What said he?   85
Ophelia
  He took me by the wrist, and held me hard;
  Then goes he to the length of all his arm,
  And, with his other hand thus o'er his brow,
  He falls to such perusal of my face
  As 'a would draw it. Long stay'd he so.   90

At last, a little shaking of mine arm,
And thrice his head thus waving up and down,
He rais'd a sigh so piteous and profound
As it did seem to shatter all his bulk
95 And end his being. That done, he lets me go,
And, with his head over his shoulder turn'd,
He seem'd to find his way without his eyes;
For out adoors he went without their helps
And to the last bended their light on me.

Polonius
100 Come, go with me. I will go seek the King.
This is the very ecstasy of love,
Whose violent property fordoes itself,
And leads the will to desperate undertakings
As oft as any passion under heaven
105 That does afflict our natures. I am sorry –
What, have you given him any hard words of
late?

Ophelia
No, my good lord; but, as you did command,
I did repel his letters, and denied
His access to me.

Polonius
That hath made him mad.
110 I am sorry that with better heed and judgment
I had not quoted him. I fear'd he did but trifle,
And meant to wreck thee; but beshrew my
jealousy!
By heaven, it is as proper to our age
To cast beyond ourselves in our opinions
115 As it is common for the younger sort
To lack discretion. Come, go we to the King.
This must be known; which, being kept close,
might move
More grief to hide than hate to utter love.
Come.

[Exeunt.]

Scene II

Elsinore. The Castle.

[Flourish. Enter KING, QUEEN, ROSENCRANTZ,
GUILDENSTERN*, and* ATTENDANTS.*]*

King
    Welcome, dear Rosencrantz and Guildenstern!
    Moreover that we much did long to see you,
    The need we have to use you did provoke
    Our hasty sending. Something have you heard
    Of Hamlet's transformation; so I call it,   5
    Sith nor th' exterior nor the inward man
    Resembles that it was. What it should be,
    More than his father's death, that thus hath
        put him
    So much from th' understanding of himself,
    I cannot deem of. I entreat you both   10
    That, being of so young days brought up with
        him,
    And sith so neighboured to his youth and
        haviour,
    That you vouchsafe your rest here in our court
    Some little time: so by your companies
    To draw him on to pleasures, and to gather,   15
    So much as from occasion you may glean,
    Whether aught to us unknown afflicts him thus
    That, open'd, lies within our remedy.
Queen
    Good gentlemen, he hath much talk'd of you;
    And sure I am two men there is not living   20
    To whom he more adheres. If it will please
        you
    To show us so much gentry and good will
    As to expend your time with us awhile
    For the supply and profit of our hope,
    Your visitation shall receive such thanks   25
    As fits a king's remembrance.

Rosencrantz

                    Both your Majesties
Might, by the sovereign power you have of us,
Put your dread pleasures more into command
Than to entreaty.

Guildenstern

               But we both obey,
30   And here give up ourselves, in the full bent,
To lay our service freely at your feet,
To be commanded.

King

Thanks, Rosencrantz and gentle Guildenstern.

Queen

Thanks, Guildenstern and gentle Rosencrantz.
35   And I beseech you instantly to visit
My too much changed son. Go, some of you,
And bring these gentlemen where Hamlet is.

Guildenstern

Heavens make our presence and our practices
Pleasant and helpful to him!

Queen

                      Aye amen!

[Exeunt ROSENCRANTZ, GUILDENSTERN, *and some*
ATTENDANTS.*]*

[Enter POLONIUS.*]*

Polonius

40   Th' ambassadors from Norway, my good lord,
Are joyfully return'd.

King

Thou still hast been the father of good news.

Polonius

Have I, my lord? I assure you, my good liege,
I hold my duty, as I hold my soul,
45   Both to my God and to my gracious King;
And I do think – or else this brain of mine
Hunts not the trail of policy so sure

As it hath us'd to do – that I have found
The very cause of Hamlet's lunacy.

King

O, speak of that; that do I long to hear.　　　　50

Polonius

Give first admittance to th' ambassadors;
My news shall be the fruit to that great feast.

King

Thyself do grace to them, and bring them in.

[Exit POLONIUS.]

He tells me, my dear Gertrude, he hath found
The head and source of all your son's
　　distemper.　　　　55

Queen

I doubt it is no other but the main,
His father's death and our o'erhasty marriage.

King

Well, we shall sift him.

[Re-enter POLONIUS, with VOLTEMAND and CORNELIUS.]

　　　　　　Welcome, my good friends!
Say, Voltemand, what from our brother
Norway?

Voltemand

Most fair return of greetings and desires.　　　　60
Upon our first, he sent out to suppress
His nephew's levies; which to him appear'd
To be a preparation 'gainst the Polack;
But, better look'd into, he truly found
It was against your Highness. Whereat griev'd,　　　　65
That so his sickness, age, and impotence,
Was falsely borne in hand, sends out arrests
On Fortinbras; which he, in brief, obeys;
Receives rebuke from Norway; and, in fine,
Makes vow before his uncle never more　　　　70
To give th' assay of arms against your Majesty.
Whereon old Norway, overcome with joy,

Gives him threescore thousand crowns in
   annual fee,
And his commission to employ those soldiers,
75   So levied as before, against the Polack;
With an entreaty, herein further shown,

[Gives a paper.]

That it might please you to give quiet pass
Through your dominions for this enterprise,
On such regards of safety and allowance
As therein are set down.
  King
80   It likes us well;
And at our more considered time we'll read,
Answer, and think upon this business.
Meantime we thank you for your well-took
   labour.
Go to your rest; at night we'll feast together.
Most welcome home!

[Exeunt AMBASSADORS *and* ATTENDANTS.*]*

  Polonius
85   This business is well ended.
My liege, and madam, to expostulate
What majesty should be, what duty is,
Why day is day, night is night, and time is time,
Were nothing, but to waste night, day, and time.
90   Therefore, since brevity is the soul of wit,
And tediousness the limbs and outward
   flourishes.
I will be brief. Your noble son is mad.
Mad call I it: for, to define true madness,
What is't but to be nothing else but mad?
But let that go.
  Queen
95   More matter with less art.
  Polonius
Madam, I swear I use no art at all.

That he's mad, 'tis true: 'tis true 'tis pity;
And pity 'tis 'tis true. A foolish figure!
But farewell it, for I will use no art.
Mad let us grant him, then; and now remains   100
That we find out the cause of this effect;
Or rather say the cause of this defect,
For this effect defective comes by cause.
Thus it remains, and the remainder thus.
Perpend.   105
I have a daughter – have while she is mine –
Who in her duty and obedience, mark,
Hath given me this. Now gather, and surmise.

[Reads.]

'To the celestial, and my soul's idol, the most
beautified Ophelia.' That's an ill phrase, a vile
phrase; 'beautified' is a vile phrase. But you shall
hear. Thus: *[Reads]* 'In her excellent white bosom,
these, etc.'
Queen
Came this from Hamlet to her?
Polonius
Good madam, stay awhile; I will be faithful.   115

[Reads.]

'Doubt thou the stars are fire;
Doubt that the sun doth move;
Doubt truth to be a liar;
But never doubt I love.

O dear Ophelia, I am ill at these numbers.
I have not art to reckon my groans; but that I
love thee best, O most best, believe it. Adieu.   120

Thine evermore, most dear lady, whilst this
machine is to him, HAMLET.'

This, in obedience, hath my daughter shown
me;

125   And more above, hath his solicitings,
       As they fell out by time, by means, and place,
       All given to mine ear.
King

                   But how hath she
       Receiv'd his love?
Polonius

               What do you think of me?
King
       As of a man faithful and honourable.
Polonius

130   I would fain prove so. But what might you think,
       When I had seen this hot love on the wing,
       As I perceiv'd it, I must tell you that,
       Before my daughter told me – what might you,
       Or my dear Majesty your queen here, think,
135   If I had play'd the desk or table-book;
       Or given my heart a winking, mute and dumb;
       Or look'd upon this love with idle sight –
       What might you think? No, I went round to work,
       And my young mistress thus I did bespeak:
140   'Lord Hamlet is a prince out of thy star;
       This must not be'. And then I prescripts gave her,
       That she should lock herself from his resort,
       Admit no messengers, receive no tokens.
       Which done, she took the fruits of my advice;
145   And he repelled, a short tale to make,
       Fell into a sadness, then into a fast,
       Thence to a watch, thence into a weakness,
       Thence to a lightness, and, by this declension,
       Into the madness wherein now he raves
       And all we mourn for.
King
150   Do you think 'tis this?
Queen
       It may be, very like.

Polonius
　　Hath there been such a time – I would fain
　　　　know that –
　　That I have positively said ''Tis so',
　　When it prov'd otherwise?

King
　　　　　　　　　　　Not that I know.

Polonius
　　Take this from this, if this be otherwise.　　　155
　　If circumstances lead me, I will find
　　Where truth is hid, though it were hid indeed
　　Within the centre.

King
　　　　　　　　How may we try it further?

Polonius
　　You know sometimes he walks four hours
　　　　together,
　　Here in the lobby.

Queen
　　　　　　　So he does, indeed.　　　160

Polonius
　　At such a time I'll loose my daughter to him.
　　Be you and I behind an arras then;
　　Mark the encounter: if he love her not,
　　And be not from his reason fall'n thereon,
　　Let me be no assistant for a state,　　　165
　　But keep a farm and carters.

King
　　　　　　　　　We will try it.

[Enter HAMLET, *reading on a book.]*

Queen
　　But look where sadly the poor wretch comes
　　　　reading.

Polonius
　　Away, I do beseech you, both away:
　　I'll board him presently. O, give me leave.

[Exeunt KING *and* QUEEN.*]*

175   How does my good Lord Hamlet?

Hamlet
Well, God-a-mercy.

Polonius
Do you know me, my lord?

Hamlet
Excellent well; you are a fish-monger.

Polonius
Not I, my lord.

Hamlet
180   Then I would you were so honest a man.

Polonius
Honest, my lord!

Hamlet
Ay, sir; to be honest, as this world goes, is to be
one man pick'd out of ten thousand.

Polonius
That's very true, my lord.

Hamlet
185   For if the sun breed maggots in a dead dog,
being a good kissing carrion – Have you a
daughter?

Polonius
I have, my lord.

Hamlet
Let her not walk i' th' sun. Conception is a
blessing. But as your daughter may conceive –
190   friend, look to't.

Polonius
How say you by that? *[Aside]* Still harping on my
daughter. Yet he knew me not at first; 'a said I
was a fishmonger. 'A is far gone, far gone. And
truly in my youth I suff'red much extremity for
love. Very near this. I'll speak to him again. –
195   What do you read, my lord?

Hamlet
Words, words, words.

Polonius
What is the matter, my lord?
Hamlet
Between who?
Polonius
I mean, the matter that you read, my lord.   200
Hamlet
Slanders, sir; for the satirical rogue says here that
old men have grey beards; that their faces are
wrinkled; their eyes purging thick amber and
plum-tree gum; and that they have a plentiful
lack of wit, together with most weak hams – all 205
which, sir, though I most powerfully and potently
believe, yet I hold it not honesty to have it thus
set down; for you yourself, sir, shall grow old as
I am, if, like a crab, you could go backward.
Polonius
[Aside] Though this be madness, yet there is 210
method in't. – Will you walk out of the air, my
lord?
Hamlet
Into my grave?
Polonius
Indeed, that's out of the air. *[Aside]*
How pregnant sometimes his replies are! a happi-
ness that often madness hits on, which reason 215
and sanity could not so prosperously be delivered
of. I will leave him, and suddenly contrive the
means of meeting between him and my daughter.
– My lord, I will take my leave of you.
Hamlet
You cannot, sir, take from me anything that I will 220
more willingly part withal – except my life, except
my life, except my life.

[Enter ROSENCRANTZ *and* GUILDENSTERN.*]*

Polonius
Fare you well, my lord.

Hamlet
These tedious old fools!
Polonius
225 You go to seek the Lord Hamlet; there he is.
Rosencrantz [To POLONIUS*]*
God save you, sir!

[Exit POLONIUS.*]*

Guildenstern
My honour'd lord!
Rosencrantz
My most dear lord!
Hamlet
My excellent good friends! How dost thou,
Guildenstern? Ah, Rosencrantz! Good lads, how
230 do you both?
Rosencrantz
As the indifferent children of the earth.
Guildenstern
Happy in that we are not over-happy;
On fortune's cap we are not the very button.
Hamlet
Nor the soles of her shoe?
Rosencrantz
235 Neither, my lord.
Hamlet
Then you live about her waist, or in the middle
of her favours?
Guildenstern
Faith, her privates we.
Hamlet
In the secret parts of Fortune? O, most true; she
is a strumpet. What news?
Rosencrantz
None, my lord, but that the world's grown
236 honest.
Hamlet
Then is doomsday near. But your news is not true.

Let me question more in particular. What have
you, my good friends, deserved at the hands of
Fortune, that she sends you to prison hither? 240
Guildenstern
Prison, my lord!
Hamlet
Denmark's a prison.
Rosencrantz
Then is the world one.
Hamlet
A goodly one; in which there are many confines,
wards, and dungeons, Denmark being one o' th'
worst. 246
Rosencrantz
We think not so, my lord.
Hamlet
Why, then, 'tis none to you; for there is nothing
either good or bad, but thinking makes it so. To
me it is a prison.
Rosencrantz
Why, then your ambition makes it one; 'tis too
narrow for your mind. 252
Hamlet
O God, I could be bounded in a nutshell and
count myself a king of infinite space, were it not
that I have bad dreams.
Guildenstern
Which dreams indeed are ambition; for the very
substance of the ambitious is merely the shadow
of a dream. 258
Hamlet
A dream itself is but a shadow.
Rosencrantz
Truly, and I hold ambition of so airy and light a
quality that it is but a shadow's shadow. 261

Hamlet

Then are our beggars bodies, and our monarchs and outstretch'd heroes the beggars' shadows. Shall we to th' court? for, by my fay, I cannot reason.

Both

265   We'll wait upon you.

Hamlet

No such matter. I will not sort you with the rest of my servants; for, to speak to you like an honest man, I am most dreadfully attended. But, in the beaten way of friendship, what make you at Elsinore?

Rosencrantz

270   To visit you, my lord; no other occasion.

Hamlet

Beggar that I am, I am even poor in thanks; but I thank you; and sure, dear friends, my thanks are too dear a half-penny. Were you not sent for? Is it your own inclining? Is it a free visitation? Come, come, deal justly with me. Come, come;

275   nay, speak.

Guildenstern

What should we say, my lord?

Hamlet

Why any thing. But to th' purpose: you were sent for; and there is a kind of confession in your looks, which your modesties have not craft enough to colour; I know the good King and

280   Queen have sent for you.

Rosencrantz

To what end, my lord?

Hamlet

That you must teach me. But let me conjure you by the rights of our fellowship, by the consonancy of our youth, by the obligation of our ever-preserved love, and by what more dear a better proposer can charge you withal, be even and direct with me, whether you were sent for or no?

Rosencrantz [Aside to GUILDENSTERN*]*
    What say you?
Hamlet [Aside]
    Nay, then, I have an eye of you, – If you love me,
    hold not off.   290
Guildenstern
    My lord, we were sent for.
Hamlet
    I will tell you why; so shall my anticipation
    prevent your discovery, and your secrecy to the
    King and Queen moult no feather. I have of late
    – but wherefore I know not – lost all my mirth,
    forgone all custom of exercises; and indeed it goes
    so heavily with my disposition that this goodly
    frame, the earth, seems to me a sterile promon-
    tory; this most excellent canopy the air, look you,
    this brave o'er-hanging firmament, this majestical
    roof fretted with golden fire – why, it appeareth
    no other thing to me than a foul and pestilent
    congregation of vapours. What a piece of work is
    a man! How noble in reason! how infinite in
    faculties! in form and moving, how express and
    admirable! in action, how like an angel! in appre-
    hension, how like a god! the beauty of the world!
    the paragon of animals! And yet, to me, what is
    this quintessence of dust? Man delights not me
    – no, nor woman neither, though by your smiling
    you seem to say so.   309
Rosencrantz
    My lord, there was no such stuff in my thoughts.
Hamlet
    Why did ye laugh, then, when I said 'Man delights
    not me'?
Rosencrantz
    To think, my lord, if you delight not in man,
    what lenten entertainment the players shall
    receive from you. We coted them on the way;
    and hither are they coming to offer you service. 316

Hamlet

He that plays the king shall be welcome – his Majesty shall have tribute on me; the adventurous knight shall use his foil and target; the lover shall not sigh gratis; the humorous man shall end his part in peace; the clown shall make those laugh whose lungs are tickle a' th' sere; and the lady shall say her mind freely, or the blank verse shall

323   halt for't. What players are they?

Rosencrantz

Even those you were wont to take such delight in – the tragedians of the city.

Hamlet

How chances it they travel? Their residence, both in reputation and profit, was better both ways.

Rosencrantz

I think their inhibition comes by the means of

329   the late innovation.

Hamlet

Do they hold the same estimation they did when I was in the city? Are they so followed?

Rosencrantz

No, indeed, are they not.

Hamlet

333   How comes it? Do they grow rusty?

Rosencrantz

Nay, their endeavour keeps in the wonted pace; but there is, sir, an eyrie of children, little eyases, that cry out on the top of question, and are most tyrannically clapp'd for't. These are now the fashion, and so berattle the common stages – so they call them – that many wearing rapiers are

340   afraid of goose quills and dare scarce come thither.

Hamlet

What, are they children? Who maintains 'em? How are they escoted? Will they pursue the quality no longer than they can sing? Will they not say afterwards, if they should grow themselves to

common players – as it is most like, if their means
are no better – their writers do them wrong to
make them exclaim against their own
succession? 347

Rosencrantz

Faith, there has been much to-do on both sides;
and the nation holds it no sin to tarre them to
controversy. There was for a while no money bid
for argument, unless the poet and the player went
to cuffs in the question. 352

Hamlet

Is't possible?

Guildenstern

O, there has been much throwing about of brains.

Hamlet

Do the boys carry it away? 355

Rosencrantz

Ay, that they do, my lord – Hercules and his
load too.

Hamlet

It is not very strange; for my uncle is King of
Denmark, and those that would make mows at
him while my father lived give twenty, forty, fifty,
a hundred ducats apiece for his picture in little. 360
'Sblood, there is something in this more than
natural, if philosophy could find it out.
[A flourish.]

Guildenstern

There are the players.

Hamlet

Gentlemen, you are welcome to Elsinore. Your
hands, come then; th' appurtenance of welcome 365
is fashion and ceremony. Let me comply with you
in this garb; lest my extent to the players, which,
I tell you, must show fairly outwards, should more
appear like entertainment than yours. You are
welcome. But my uncle-father and aunt-mother
are deceived. 370

Guildenstern
In what, my dear lord?
Hamlet
I am but mad north-north-west; when the wind
is southerly I know a hawk from a handsaw.

[Re-enter POLONIUS.]

Polonius
Well be with you, gentlemen!
Hamlet
375 Hark you, Guildenstern, and you too – at each
ear a hearer: that great baby you see there is not
yet out of his swaddling clouts.
Rosencrantz
Happily he is the second time come to them; for
they say an old man is twice a child.
Hamlet
380 I will prophesy he comes to tell me of the players;
mark it. You say right, sir: a Monday morning;
'twas then indeed.
Polonius
My lord, I have news to tell you.
Hamlet
385 My lord, I have news to tell you. When Roscius
was an actor in Rome –
Polonius
The actors are come hither, my lord.
Hamlet
Buzz, buzz!
Polonius
Upon my honour –
Hamlet
Then came each actor on his ass –
Polonius
390 The best actors in the world, either for tragedy,
comedy, history, pastoral, pastoral-comical,
historical-pastoral, tragical-historical, tragical-
comical-historical-pastoral, scene individable, or

poem unlimited. Seneca cannot be too heavy nor
Plautus too light. For the law of writ and the
liberty, these are the only men.   395

Hamlet
 O Jephthah, judge of Israel, what a treasure hadst
 thou!

Polonious
 What a treasure had he, my lord?

Hamlet
 Why –

  'One fair daughter, and no more,
  The which he loved passing well'.   400

Polonius [Aside]
 Still on my daughter.

Hamlet
 Am I not i' th' right, old Jephthah?

Polonius
 If you call me Jephthah, my lord, I have a
  daughter that I love passing well.

Hamlet
 Nay, that follows not.   405

Polonius
 What follows then, my lord?

Hamlet
 Why –

  'As by lot, god wot'

 and then, you know,

  'It came to pass, as most like it was'.

The first row of the pious chanson will show you
more; for look where my abridgement comes.   410

[Enter the PLAYERS.*]*

You are welcome, masters; welcome, all. – I am
glad to see thee well. – Welcome, good friends.
– O, my old friend! Why thy face is valanc'd since

I saw thee last; com'st thou to beard me in Denmark? – What, my young lady and mistress! By'r lady, your ladyship is nearer to heaven than when I saw you last by the altitude of a chopine. Pray God, your voice, like a piece of uncurrent gold, be not crack'd within the ring. – Masters, you are all welcome. We'll e'en to't like French falconers, fly at anything we see. We'll have a speech straight. Come, give us a taste of your quality; come, a passionate speech.

1 Player
What speech, my good lord?

Hamlet

425   I heard thee speak me a speech once, but it was never acted; or, if it was, not above once; for the play, I remember, pleas'd not the million; 'twas caviary to the general. But it was – as I received it, and others whose judgments in such matters cried in the top of mine – an excellent play, well disgested in the scenes, set down with as much modesty as cunning. I remember one said there were no sallets in the lines to make the matter savoury, nor no matter in the phrase that might indict the author of affectation; but call'd it an honest method, as wholesome as sweet, and very much more handsome than fine. One speech in it I chiefly lov'd: 'twas [neas' tale to Dido; and thereabout of it especially where he speaks of Priam's slaughter. If it live in your memory, begin at this line – let me see, let me see:
'The rugged Pyrrhus, like th' Hyrcanian beast,'
'Tis not so; it begins with Pyrrhus.

445   'The rugged Pyrrhus, he whose sable arms,
Black as his purpose, did the night resemble
When he lay couched in the ominous horse,
Hath now this dread and black complexion
      smear'd
With heraldry more dismal; head to foot

Now is he total gules, horridly trick'd   450
With blood of fathers, mothers, daughters, sons,
Bak'd and impasted with the parching streets,
That lend a tyrannous and damned light
To their lord's murder. Roasted in wrath and
   fire,
And thus o'er-sized with coagulate gore,   455
With eyes like carbuncles, the hellish Pyrrhus
Old grandsire Priam seeks.'
So proceed you.

Polonius

For God, my lord, well spoken, with good accent
and good discretion.   460

1 Player

'Anon he finds him
Striking too short at Greeks; his antique sword,
Rebellious to his arm, lies where it falls,
Repugnant to command. Unequal match'd,
Pyrrhus at Priam drives, in rage strikes wide;   465
But with the whiff and wind of his fell sword
Th' unnerved father falls. Then senseless Ilium,
Seeming to feel this blow, with flaming top
Stoops to his base, and with a hideous crash
Takes prisoner Pyrrhus' ear. For lo! his sword,   470
Which was declining on the milky head
Of reverend Priam, seem'd i' th' air to stick.
So, as a painted tyrant. Pyrrhus stood
And, like a neutral to his will and matter,
Did nothing.   475
But as we often see, against some storm,
A silence in the heavens, the rack stand still,
The bold winds speechless, and the orb below
As hush as death, anon the dreadful thunder
Doth rend the region; so, after Pyrrhus' pause,   480
A roused vengeance sets him new a-work;
And never did the Cyclops' hammers fall
On Mars's armour, forg'd for proof eterne,
With less remorse than Pyrrhus' bleeding sword

485   Now falls on Priam.
        Out, out, thou strumpet, Fortune! All you gods,
        In general synod, take away her power;
        Break all the spokes and fellies from her wheel,
        And bowl the round nave down the hill of
            heaven,
490   As low as to the fiends.'
        Polonius
        This is too long.
        Hamlet
        It shall to the barber's, with your beard.
        Prithee say on. He's for a jig, or a tale of bawdry,
        or he sleeps. Say on; come to Hecuba.
        1 Player
495   'But who, ah, who had seen the mobled queen –'
        Hamlet
        'The mobled queen'?
        Polonius
        That's good; 'mobled queen' is good.
        1 Player
        'Run barefoot up and down, threat'ning the
            flames
        With bisson rheum; a clout upon that head
500   Where late the diadem stood, and for a robe,
        About her lank and all o'er-teemed lions,
        A blanket, in the alarm of fear caught up –
        Who this had seen, with tongue in venom
            steep'd,
        'Gainst Fortune's state would treason have
            pronounc'd.
505   But if the gods themselves did see her then,
        When she saw Pyrrhus make malicious sport
        In mincing with his sword her husband's limbs,
        The instant burst of clamour that she made –
        Unless things mortal move them not at all –
        Would have made milch the burning eyes of
510   heaven,
        And passion in the gods.'

Polonius
> Look whe'er he has not turn'd his colour, and
> has tears in 's eyes. Prithee no more.

Hamlet
> 'Tis well; I'll have thee speak out the rest of this
> soon. – Good my lord, will you see the players 515
> well bestowed? Do you hear: let them be well
> used; for they are the abstract and brief chronicles
> of the time; after your death you were better have
> a bad epitaph than their ill report while you live.

Polonius
> My lord, I will use them according to their desert. 520

Hamlet
> God's bodykins, man, much better. Use every man
> after his desert, and who shall scape whipping?
> Use them after your own honour and dignity: the
> less they deserve, the more merit is in your bounty.
> Take them in. 525

Polonius
> Come, sirs.

Hamlet
> Follow him, friends. We'll hear a play to-morrow.
> Dost thou hear me, old friend; can you play 'The
> Murder of Gonzago'?

1 Player
> Ay, my lord. 530

Hamlet
> We'll ha't to-morrow night. You could, for a need,
> study a speech of some dozen or sixteen lines
> which I would set down and insert in't, could
> you not?

1 Player
> Ay, my lord. 537

Hamlet
> Very well. Follow that lord; and look you mock
> him not. *[Exeunt* POLONIUS *and* PLAYERS*]* My good
> friends, I'll leave you till night. You are welcome
> to Elsinore.

Rosencrantz
540　Good my lord!

　　　[Exeunt ROSENCRANTZ *and* GUILDENSTERN.*]*

Hamlet
　　Ay, so God buy to you! Now I am alone.
　　O, what a rogue and peasant slave am I!
　　Is it not monstrous that this player here,
　　But in a fiction, in a dream of passion,
545　Could force his soul so to his own conceit
　　That from her working all his visage wann'd;
　　Tears in his eyes, distraction in's aspect,
　　A broken voice, and his whole function suiting
　　With forms to his conceit? And all for nothing!
550　For Hecuba!
　　What's Hecuba to him or he to Hecuba,
　　That he should weep for her? What would he
　　　　do,
　　Had he the motive and the cue for passion
　　That I have? He would drown the stage with
　　　　tears,
555　And cleave the general ear with horrid speech;
　　Make mad the guilty, and appal the free,
　　Confound the ignorant, and amaze indeed
　　The very faculties of eyes and ears.
　　Yet I,
560　A dull and muddy-mettl'd rascal, peak,
　　Like John-a-dreams, unpregnant of my cause,
　　And can say nothing; no, not for a king
　　Upon whose property and most dear life
　　A damn'd defeat was made. Am I a coward?
565　Who calls me villain, breaks my pate across,
　　Plucks off my beard and blows it in my face,
　　Tweaks me by the nose, gives me the lie i' th'
　　　　throat
　　As deep as to the lungs? Who does me this?
　　Ha!
570　'Swounds, I should take it; for it cannot be

But I am pigeon-liver'd and lack gall
To make oppression bitter, or ere this
I should 'a fatted all the region kites
With this slave's offal. Bloody, bawdy villain!   575
Remorseless, treacherous, lecherous, kindless
   villain!
O, vengeance!
Why, what an ass am I! This is most brave,
That I, the son of a dear father murder'd,
Prompted to my revenge by heaven and hell,   580
Must, like a whore, unpack my heart with
   words,
And fall a-cursing like a very drab,
A scullion! Fie upon't! foh!
About, my brains. Hum – I have heard
That guilty creatures, sitting at a play,
Have by the very cunning of the scene   585
Been struck so to the soul that presently
They have proclaim'd their malefactions;
For murder, though it have no tongue, will
   speak
With most miraculous organ. I'll have these
   players
Play something like the murder of my father   590
Before mine uncle. I'll observe his looks;
I'll tent him to the quick. If 'a do blench,
I know my course. The spirit that I have seen
May be a devil; and the devil hath power
T'assume a pleasing shape; yea, and perhaps   595
Out of my weakness and my melancholy,
As he is very potent with such spirits,
Abuses me to damn me. I'll have grounds
More relative than this. The play's the thing
Wherein I'll catch the conscience of the King.   600

[Exit.]

ACT THREE
Scene I

Elsinore. The Castle.

[Enter KING, QUEEN, POLONIUS, OPHELIA, ROSENCRANTZ,
and GUILDENSTERN.*]*

King
    And can you by no drift of conference
    Get from him why he puts on this confusion,
    Grating so harshly all his days of quiet
    With turbulent and dangerous lunacy?

Rosencrantz
5   He does confess he feels himself distracted,
    But from what cause 'a will by no means speak.

Guildenstern
    Nor do we find him forward to be sounded;
    But, with a crafty madness, keeps aloof
    When we would bring him on to some
        confession
    Of his true state.

Queen
10   Did he receive you well?

Rosencrantz
    Most like a gentleman.

Guildenstern
    But with much forcing of his disposition.

Rosencrantz
    Niggard of question; but of our demands
    Most free in his reply.

Queen
                 Did you assay him
15   To any pastime?

Rosencrantz
    Madam, it so fell out that certain players
    We o'er-raught on the way. Of these we told him;

And there did seem in him a kind of joy
To hear of it. They are here about the court,
And, as I think, they have already order   20
This night to play before him.
Polonius
       'Tis most true;
And he beseech'd me to entreat your Majesties
To hear and see the matter.
King
With all my heart; and it doth much content me
To hear him so inclin'd.   25
Good gentlemen, give him a further edge,
And drive his purpose into these delights.
Rosencrantz
We shall, my lord.

  [Exeunt ROSENCRANTZ *and* GUILDENSTERN.*]*

King
      Sweet Gertrude, leave us too;
For we have closely sent for Hamlet hither,
That he, as 'twere by accident, may here   30
Affront Ophelia.
Her father and myself – lawful espials –
Will so bestow ourselves that, seeing unseen,
We may of their encounter frankly judge,
And gather by him, as he is behav'd,   35
If't be th' affliction of his love or no
That thus he suffers for.
Queen
      I shall obey you;
And for your part, Ophelia, I do wish
That your good beauties be the happy cause
Of Hamlet's wildness; so shall I hope your
 virtues   40
Will bring him to his wonted way again,
To both your honours.
Ophelia
     Madam, I wish it may.

[Exit QUEEN.*]*

Polonius
    Ophelia, walk you here. – Gracious, so please you,
    We will bestow ourselves. – Read on this book;
45   That show of such an exercise may colour
    Your loneliness. – We are oft to blame in this:
    'Tis too much prov'd, that with devotion's visage
    And pious action we do sugar o'er
    The devil himself.
King [Aside]
                O, 'tis too true!
    How smart a lash that speech doth give my
50   conscience!
    The harlot's cheek, beautied with plast'ring art,
    Is not more ugly to the thing that helps it
    Than is my deed to my most painted word.
    O heavy burden!
Polonius
55   I hear him coming; let's withdraw, my lord.

[Exeunt KING *and* POLONIUS.*]*

[Enter HAMLET.*]*

Hamlet
    To be, or not to be – that is the question;
    Whether 'tis nobler in the mind to suffer
    The slings and arrows of outrageous fortune,
    Or to take arms against a sea of troubles,
60   And by opposing end them? To die, to sleep –
    No more; and by a sleep to say we end
    The heart-ache and the thousand natural shocks
    That flesh is heir to. 'Tis a consummation
    Devoutly to be wish'd. To die, to sleep;
65   To sleep, perchance to dream. Ay, there's the rub;
    For in that sleep of death what dreams may come,
    When we have shuffled off this mortal coil,

Must give us pause. There's the respect
That makes calamity of so long life;
For who would bear the whips and scorns of
    time,   70
Th' oppressor's wrong, the proud man's
    contumely,
The pangs of despis'd love, the law's delay,
The insolence of office, and the spurns
That patient merit of th' unworthy takes,
When he himself might his quietus make   75
With a bare bodkin? Who would these fardels
    bear,
To grunt and sweat under a weary life,
But that the dread of something after death –
The undiscover'd country, from whose bourn
No traveller returns – puzzles the will,   80
And makes us rather bear those ills we have
Than fly to others that we know not of?
Thus conscience does make cowards of us all;
And thus the native hue of resolution
Is sicklied o'er with the pale cast of thought,   85
And enterprises of great pitch and moment,
With this regard, their currents turn awry
And lose the name of action. – Soft you now!
The fair Ophelia. – Nymph, in thy orisons
Be all my sins rememb'red.
Ophelia

                         Good my lord,   90
How does your honour for this many a day?
Hamlet
    I humbly thank you; well, well, well.
Ophelia
    My lord, I have remembrances of yours
    That I have longed long to re-deliver.
    I pray you now receive them.
Hamlet
                        No, not I;   95
    I never gave you aught.

Ophelia
My honour'd lord, you know right well you
  did,
And with them words of so sweet breath
  compos'd
As made the things more rich; their perfume
  lost,
100 Take these again; for to the noble mind
Rich gifts wax poor when givers prove unkind.
There, my lord.

Hamlet
Ha, ha! Are you honest?

Ophelia
My lord?

Hamlet
105 Are you fair?

Ophelia
What means your lordship?

Hamlet
That if you be honest and fair, your honesty
should admit no discourse to your beauty.

Ophelia
Could beauty, my lord, have better commerce
110 than with honesty?

Hamlet
Ay, truly; for the power of beauty will sooner
transform honesty from what it is to a bawd than
the force of honesty can translate beauty into his
likeness. This was sometime a paradox, but now
115 the time gives it proof. I did love you once.

Ophelia
Indeed, my lord, you made me believe so.

Hamlet
You should not have believ'd me; for virtue cannot
so inoculate our old stock but we shall relish of
it. I loved you not.

Ophelia
120 I was the more deceived.

Hamlet

Get thee to a nunnery. Why wouldst thou be a breeder of sinners? I am myself indifferent honest, but yet I could accuse me of such things that it were better my mother had not borne me: I am very proud, revengeful, ambitious; with more offences at my beck than I have thoughts to put them in, imagination to give them shape, or time to act them in. What should such fellows as I do crawling between earth and heaven? We are arrant knaves, all; believe none of us. Go thy ways to a nunnery. Where's your father?   130

Ophelia

At home, my lord.

Hamlet

Let the doors be shut upon him, that he may play the fool nowhere but in's own house. Farewell.

Ophelia

O, help him, you sweet heavens!   134

Hamlet

If thou dost marry, I'll give thee this plague for thy dowry: be thou as chaste as ice, as pure as snow, thou shalt not escape calumny. Get thee to a nunnery, go, farewell. Or, if thou wilt needs marry, marry a fool; for wise men know well enough what monsters you make of them. To a nunnery, go; and quickly too. Farewell.   140

Ophelia

O heavenly powers, restore him!

Hamlet

I have heard of your paintings too, well enough; God hath given you one face, and you make yourselves another. You jig and amble, and you lisp, and nickname God's creatures, and make your wantonness your ignorance. Go to, I'll no more on't; it hath made me mad. I say we will have no moe marriage: those that are married

already, all but one, shall live; the rest shall keep
as they are. To a nunnery, go.

[Exit.]

Ophelia

150   O, what a noble mind is here o'er-thrown!
The courtier's, soldier's, scholar's, eye, tongue,
    sword;
Th' expectancy and rose of the fair state,
The glass of fashion and the mould of form,
Th' observ'd of all observers – quite, quite
    down!
155   And I, of ladies most deject and wretched,
That suck'd the honey of his music vows,
Now see that noble and most sovereign reason,
Like sweet bells jangled, out of time and harsh;
That unmatch'd form and feature of blown
    youth
160   Blasted with ecstasy, O, woe is me
T' have seen what I have seen, see what I see!

[Re-enter KING *and* POLONIUS.*]*

King

Love! His affections do not that way tend;
Nor what he spake, though it lack'd form a
    little,
Was not like madness. There's something in his
    soul
165   O'er which his melancholy sits on brood;
And I do doubt the hatch and the disclose
Will be some danger; which to prevent
I have in quick determination
Thus set it down: he shall with speed to
    England
170   For the demand of our neglected tribute.
Haply the seas and countries different,
With variable objects, shall expel
This something-settled matter in his heart

Whereon his brains still beating puts him thus
From fashion of himself. What think you on't?   175

Polonius

It shall do well. But yet do I believe
The origin and commencement of his grief
Sprung from neglected love. How now, Ophelia!
You need not tell us what Lord Hamlet said;
We heard it all. My lord, do as you please;   180
But if you hold it fit, after the play
Let his queen mother all alone entreat him
To show his grief. Let her be round with him;
And I'll be plac'd, so please you, in the ear
Of all their conference. If she find him not,   185
To England send him; or confine him where
Your wisdom best shall think.

King

It shall be so:
Madness in great ones must not unwatch'd go.

[Exeunt.]

Scene II

Elsinore. The Castle.

[Enter HAMLET *and three of the* PLAYERS.*]*

Hamlet

Speak the speech, I pray you, as I pronounc'd it to you, trippingly on the tongue; but if you mouth it, as many of our players do, I had as lief the town-crier spoke my lines. Nor do not saw the air too much with your hand, thus, but use all gently; for in the very torrent, tempest, and, as I may say, whirlwind of your passion, you must acquire and beget a temperance that may give it smoothness. O, it offends me to the soul to hear a robustious periwig-pated fellow tear a passion to tatters, to very rags, to split the ears of the groundlings, who, for the most part, are capable of nothing but inexplicable dumb shows and noise. I would have such a fellow whipp'd for o'erdoing Termagant; it out-herods Herod. Pray you avoid it.

14

1 Player

I warrant your honour.

Hamlet

Be not too tame neither, but let your own discretion be your tutor. Suit the action to the word, the word to the action; with this special observance, that you o'er-step not the modesty of nature; for any-thing so o'erdone is from the purpose of playing, whose end, both at the first and now, was and is to hold, as 'twere, the mirror up to nature; to show virtue her own feature, scorn her own image, and the very age and body of the time his form and pressure. Now, this overdone or come tardy off, though it makes the unskilful laugh, cannot but make the judicious grieve; the censure of the which one must, in your allowance, o'erweight a whole theatre of others. O, there be players that I have seen play – and heard others praise, and that highly – not to speak it profanely, that, neither having th' accent of Christians, nor the gait of Christian, pagan, nor man, have so strutted and bellowed that I have thought some of Nature's journeymen had made men, and not made them well, they imitated humanity so abominably.   34

1 Player

I hope we have reform'd that indifferently with us, sir.

Hamlet

O, reform it altogether. And let those that play your clowns speak no more than is set down for them; for there be of them that will themselves laugh, to set on some quantity of barren spectators to laugh too, though in the meantime some necessary question of the play be then to be considered. That's villainous, and shows a most pitiful ambition in the fool that uses it. Go, make you ready.

[Exeunt PLAYERS.*]*

[Enter POLONIUS, ROSENCRANTZ, *and* GUILDENSTERN.*]*

How now, my lord! Will the King hear this piece of work?   45

Polonius

And the Queen too, and that presently.

Hamlet

Bid the players make haste.

[Exit POLONIUS.*]*

Will you two help to hasten them?

Rosencrantz

Ay, my lord.

[Exeunt they two.]

Hamlet
50   What, ho, Horatio!

[Enter HORATIO.*]*

Horatio
    Here, sweet lord, at your service,
Hamlet
    Horatio, thou art e'en as just a man
    As e'er my conversation cop'd withal.
Horatio
    O my dear lord!
Hamlet
                    Nay, do not think I flatter;
55   For what advancement may I hope from thee,
    That no revenue hast but thy good spirits
    To feed and clothe thee? Why should the poor
        be flatter'd?
    No, let the candied tongue lick absurd pomp,
    And crook the pregnant hinges of the knee
    Where thrift may follow fawning. Dost thou
60   hear?
    Since my dear soul was mistress of her choice
    And could of men distinguish her election,
    Sh'hath seal'd thee for herself; for thou hast been
    As one in suff'ring all, that suffers nothing;
65   A man that Fortune's buffets and rewards
    Hast ta'en with equal thanks; and blest are those
    Whose blood and judgment are so well
        comeddled
    That they are not a pipe for Fortune's finger
    To sound what stop she please. Give me that
        man
70   That is not passion's slave, and I will wear him
    In my heart's core, ay, in my heart of heart,
    As I do thee. Something too much of this.
    There is a play to-night before the King;
    One scene of it comes near the circumstance
75   Which I have told thee of my father's death.

I prithee, when thou seest that act afoot,
Even with the very comment of thy soul
Observe my uncle. If his occulted guilt
Do not itself unkennel in one speech,
It is a damned ghost that we have seen,   80
And my imaginations are as foul
As Vulcan's stithy. Give him heedful note;
For I mine eyes will rivet to his face;
And, after, we will both our judgments join
In censure of his seeming.

Horatio

                Well, my lord.   85
If 'a steal aught the whilst this play is playing,
And scape detecting, I will pay the theft.

*[Enter trumpets and kettledrums. Danish march. Sound
a flourish. Enter* KING, QUEEN, POLONIUS, OPHELIA,
ROSENCRANTZ, GUILDENSTERN, *and other* LORDS *attendant,
with the* GUARD *carrying torches.]*

Hamlet

They are coming to the play; I must be idle.
Get you a place.

King

How fares our cousin Hamlet?   90

Hamlet

Excellent, i' faith; of the chameleon's dish. I eat the
air, promise-cramm'd; you cannot feed capons so.

King

I have nothing with this answer, Hamlet; these
words are not mine.   94

Hamlet

No, nor mine now. *[To* POLONIUS*]* My lord, you
play'd once i' th' university, you say?

Polonius

That did I, my lord, and was accounted a good
actor.

Hamlet

What did you enact?   99

Polonius
    I did enact Julius Caesar; I was kill'd i' th' Capitol;
    Brutus kill'd me.
Hamlet
    It was a brute part of him to kill so capital a calf
    there. Be the players ready?
Rosencrantz
    Ay, my lord; they stay upon your patience.
Queen
105   Come hither, my dear Hamlet, sit by me.
Hamlet
    No, good mother, here's metal more attractive.
Polonius [To the KING]
    O, ho! do you mark that?
Hamlet
    Lady, shall I lie in your lap?

            [Lying down at OPHELIA's *feet.]*

Ophelia
    No, my lord.
Hamlet
110   I mean, my head upon your lap?
Ophelia
    Ay, my lord.
Hamlet
    Do you think I meant country matters?
Ophelia
    I think nothing, my lord.
Hamlet
    That's a fair thought to lie between maids' legs.
Ophelia
115   What is, my lord?
Hamlet
    Nothing.
Ophelia
    You are merry, my lord.
Hamlet
    Who, I?

Ophelia

Ay, my lord.   119

Hamlet

O God, your only jig-maker! What should a man
do but be merry? For look you how cheerfully
my mother looks, and my father died within's
two hours.

Ophelia

Nay, 'tis twice two months, my lord.   123

Hamlet

So long? Nay then, let the devil wear black, for
I'll have a suit of sables. O heavens! die two months
ago, and not forgotten yet? Then there's hope a
great man's memory may outlive his life half a
year; but, by'r lady, 'a must build churches, then;
or else shall 'a suffer not thinking on, with the
hobby-horse, whose epitaph is 'For O, for O,
the hobby-horse is forgot!'   130

*[The trumpet sounds. Hautboys play. The Dumb Show
enters.]*

*[Enter a King and a Queen, very lovingly; the Queen
embracing him and he her. She kneels, and makes show
of protestation unto him. He takes her up, and declines
his head upon her neck. He lies him down upon a bank of
flowers; she, seeing him asleep, leaves him. Anon comes in
a Fellow, takes off his crown, kisses it, pours poison in the
sleeper's ears, and leaves him. The Queen returns; finds
the King dead, and makes passionate action. The Poisoner,
with some two or three Mutes, comes in again, seeming to
condole with her. The dead body is carried away. The Poisoner woos the Queen with gifts; she seems harsh awhile,
but in the end accepts his love.]*

[Exeunt.]

Ophelia

What means this, my lord?

Hamlet
Marry, this is miching mallecho; it means mischief.
Ophelia
135   Belike this show imports the argument of the play.

[Enter Prologue.]

Hamlet
We shall know by this fellow: the players cannot keep counsel; they'll tell all.
Ophelia
138   Will 'a tell us what this show meant?
Hamlet
Ay, or any show that you will show him.
Be not you asham'd to show, he'll not shame to
141   tell you what it means.
Ophelia
You are naught, you are naught. I'll mark the play.
Prologue
For us, and for our tragedy,
145   *Here stooping to your clemency,*
We beg your hearing patiently.

[Exit.]

Hamlet
Is this a prologue, or the posy of a ring?
Ophelia
'Tis brief, my lord.
Hamlet
As woman's love.

[Enter the PLAYER KING and QUEEN.]

Player King
150   *Full thirty times hath Phoebus' cart gone round*
Neptune's salt wash and Tellus' orbed ground,
And thirty dozen moons with borrowed sheen
About the world have times twelve thirties been,
Since love our hearts and Hymen did our hands
155   *Unit comutual in most sacred bands.*

Player Queen

So many journeys may the sun and moon
Make us again count o'er ere love be done!
But, woe is me, you are so sick of late,
So far from cheer and from your former state,
That I distrust you. Yet, though I distrust,   160
Discomfort you, my lord, it nothing must;
For women fear too much even as they love,
And women's fear and love hold quantity,
In neither aught, or in extremity.
Now, what my love is, proof hath made you know;   165
And as my love is siz'd, my fear is so.
Where love is great, the littlest doubts are fear;
Where little fears grow great, great love grows
   there.

Player King

Faith, I must leave thee, love, and shortly too:
My operant powers their functions leave to do;   170
And thou shalt live in this fair world behind,
Honour'd, belov'd; and haply one as kind
For husband shalt thou —

Player Queen

                              O, confound the rest!
Such love must needs be treason in my breast.
In second husband let me be accurst!   175
None wed the second but who kill'd the first.

Hamlet

That's wormwood, wormwood.

Player Queen

The instances that second marriage move
Are base respects of thrift, but none of love.
A second time I kill my husband dead,   180
When second husband kisses me in bed.

Player King

I do believe you think what now you speak;
But what we do determine oft we break.
Purpose is but the slave to memory,
Of violent birth, but poor validity;   185

Which now, the fruit unripe, sticks on the tree;
But fall unshaken when they mellow be.
Most necessary 'tis that we forget
To pay ourselves what to ourselves is debt.
190   What to ourselves in passion we propose,
The passion ending, doth the purpose lose.
The violence of either grief or joy
Their own enactures with themselves destroy.
Where joy most revels grief doth most lament;
195   Grief joys, joy grieves, on slender accident.
This world is not for aye; nor 'tis not strange
That even our loves should with our fortunes
    change;
For 'tis a question left us yet to prove,
Whether love lead fortune or else fortune love.
200   The great man down, you mark his favourite flies;
The poor advanc'd makes friends of enemies.
And hitherto doth love on fortune tend;
For who not needs shall never lack a friend,
And who in want a hollow friend doth try,
205   Directly seasons him his enemy.
But, orderly to end where I begun,
Our wills and fates do so contrary run
That our devices still are overthrown;
Our thoughts are ours, their ends none of our own.
210   So think thou wilt no second husband wed;
But die thy thoughts when thy first lord is dead.

Player Queen

Nor earth to me give food, nor heaven light,
Sport and repose lock from me day and night,
To desperation turn my trust and hope,
215   An anchor's cheer in prison be my scope,
Each opposite that blanks the face of joy
Meet what I would have well, and it destroy,
Both here and hence pursue me lasting strife,
If, once a widow, ever I be wife!

Hamlet

220   If she should break it now!

Player King
> 'Tis deeply sworn. Sweet, leave me here awhile;
> My spirits grow dull, and fain I would beguile
> The tedious day with sleep.

[Sleeps.]

Player Queen
>   Sleep rock thy brain,
> And never come mischance between us twain!

[Exit.]

Hamlet
> Madam, how like you this play?   225

Queen
> The lady doth protest too much, methinks.

Hamlet
> O, but she'll keep her word.

King
> Have you heard the argument? Is there no offence
> in't?

Hamlet
> No, no; they do but jest, poison in jest; no offence
> i' th' world.   230

King
> What do you call the play?

Hamlet
> 'The Mouse-trap.' Marry, how? Tropically. This
> play is the image of a murder done in Vienna:
> Gonzago is the duke's name; his wife, Baptista.
> You shall see anon. 'Tis a knavish piece of work; 235
> but what of that? Your Majesty, and we that have
> free souls, it touches us not. Let the galled jade
> wince, our withers are unwrung.

[Enter LUCIANUS.]

> This is one Lucianus, nephew to the King.

Ophelia
> You are as good as a chorus, my lord.   240

Hamlet
I could interpret between you and your love, if I
could see the puppets dallying.

Ophelia
You are keen, my lord, you are keen.

Hamlet
It would cost you a groaning to take off mine edge.

Ophelia
245   Still better, and worse.

Hamlet
So you mis-take your husbands. – Begin, murderer;
pox, leave thy damnable faces and begin. Come;
the croaking raven doth bellow for revenge.

Lucianus
   Thoughts black, hands apt, drugs fit, and time
     agreeing;
250   *Confederate season, else no creature seeing;*
   Thou mixture rank, of midnight weeds collected,
   With Hecat's ban thrice blasted, thrice infected,
   Thy natural magic and dire property
254   *On wholesome life usurps immediately.*

[Pours the poison in his ears.]

Hamlet
'A poisons him i' th' garden for his estate. His
name's Gonzago. The story is extant, and written
in very choice Italian. You shall see anon how
the murderer gets the love of Gonzago's wife.

Ophelia
The King rises.

Hamlet
260   What, frighted with false fire!

Queen
How fares my lord?

Polonius
Give o'er the play.

King
Give me some light. Away!

Polonius
Lights, lights, lights!

[Exeunt all but HAMLET *and* HORATIO.*]*

Hamlet
Why, let the strucken deer go weep,   265
The hart ungalled play;
For some must watch, while some must sleep;
    Thus runs the world away.
Would not this, sir, and a forest of feathers – if
the rest of my fortunes turn Turk with me – with 270
two Provincial roses on my raz'd shoes, get me a
fellowship in a cry of players, sir?
Horatio
Half a share.
Hamlet
A whole one, I.

For thou dost know, O Damon dear,   274
This realm dismantled was
Of Jove himself; and now reigns here
A very, very – paiock.

Horatio
You might have rhym'd.
Hamlet
O good Horatio, I'll take the ghost's word for a
thousand pound. Didst perceive?   281
Horatio
Very well, my lord.
Hamlet
Upon the talk of the poisoning.
Horatio
I did very well note him.
Hamlet
Ah, ha! Come, some music. Come, the recorders. 286
For if the King like not the comedy,
Why, then, belike he likes it not, perdy.
Come, some music.

[Re-enter ROSENCRANTZ *and* GUILDENSTERN.*]*

Guildenstern
Good my lord, vouchsafe me a word with you.
Hamlet
290   Sir, a whole history.
Guildenstern
The King, sir –
Hamlet
Ay, sir, what of him?
Guildenstern
Is, in his retirement, marvellous distemp'red.
Hamlet
With drink, sir?
Guildenstern
295   No, my lord, rather with choler.
Hamlet
Your wisdom should show itself more richer to
signify this to his doctor; for for me to put him
to his purgation would perhaps plunge him into
far more choler.
Guildenstern
Good my lord, put your discourse into some
301   frame, and start not so wildly from my affair.
Hamlet
I am tame, sir. Pronounce.
Guildenstern
The Queen, your mother, in most great affliction
of spirit, hath sent me to you.
Hamlet
305   You are welcome.
Guildenstern
Nay, good my lord, this courtesy is not of the
right breed. If it shall please you to make me a
wholesome answer, I will do your mother's
commandment; if not, your pardon and my return
310   shall be the end of my business.
Hamlet
Sir, I cannot.

Rosencrantz
    What, my lord?
Hamlet
    Make you a wholesome answer; my wit's diseas'd.
    But, sir, such answer as I can make, you shall
    command; or rather, as you say, my mother.
    Therefore no more, but to the matter: my mother,
    you say –   316
Rosencrantz
    Then thus she says: your behaviour hath struck
    her into amazement and admiration.
Hamlet
    O wonderful son, that can so stonish a mother!
    But is there no sequel at the heels of this mother's
    admiration? Impart.   321
Rosencrantz
    She desires to speak with you in her closet ere
    you go to bed.
Hamlet
    We shall obey, were she ten times our mother.
    Have you any further trade with us?   325
Rosencrantz
    My lord, your once did love me.
Hamlet
    And do still, by these pickers and stealers.
Rosencrantz
    Good my lord, what is your cause of distemper?
    You do surely bar the door upon your own liberty,
    if you deny your griefs to your friend.   330
Hamlet
    Sir, I lack advancement.
Rosencrantz
    How can that be, when you have the voice of the
    King himself for your succession in Denmark?   333
Hamlet
    Ay, sir, but 'While the grass grows' – the proverb
    is something musty.

        [Re-enter the PLAYERS, *with recorders.]*

O, the recorders! Let me see one. To withdraw with you – why do you go about to recover the wind of me, as if you would drive me into a toil?

Guildenstern

340   O my lord, if my duty be too bold, my love is too unmannerly.

Hamlet

I do not well understand that. Will you play upon this pipe?

Guildenstern

My lord, I cannot.

Hamlet

345   I pray you.

Guildenstern

Believe me, I cannot.

Hamlet

I do beseech you.

Guildenstern

I know no touch of it, my lord.

Hamlet

It is as easy as lying: govern these ventages with your fingers and thumb, give it breath with your
351   mouth, and it will discourse most eloquent music. Look you, these are the stops.

Guildenstern

353   But these cannot I command to any utterance of harmony; I have not the skill.

Hamlet

Why, look you now, how unworthy a thing you make of me! You would play upon me; you would seem to know my stops; you would pluck out the heart of my mystery; you would sound me from my lowest note to the top of my compass; and there is much music, excellent voice, in this little organ, yet cannot you make it speak. 'Sblood, do you think I am easier to be play'd on than a pipe? Call me what instrument you will, though you can fret me, yet you cannot play upon me.

[Re-enter POLONIUS.]

God bless you, sir!

Polonius

My lord, the Queen would speak with you, and 365
presently.

Hamlet

Do you see yonder cloud that's almost in shape
of a camel?

Polonius

By th' mass, and 'tis like a camel indeed.

Hamlet

Methinks it is like a weasel.   370

Polonius

It is back'd like a weasel.

Hamlet

Or like a whale?

Polonius

Very like a whale.

Hamlet

Then I will come to my mother by and by. *[Aside]*
They fool me to the top of my bendt. – I will
come by and by.   375

Polonius

I will say so.

[Exit POLONIUS.]

Hamlet

'By and by' is easily said. Leave me, friends.

[Exeunt all but HAMLET.]

'Tis now the very witching time of night,
When churchyards yawn, and hell itself
     breathes out
Contagion to this world. Now could I drink hot
     blood,   380
And do such bitter business as the day
Would quake to look on. Soft! now to my
     mother.

O heart, lose not thy nature; let not ever
The soul of Nero enter this firm bosom.
385   Let me be cruel, not unnatural:
I will speak daggers to her, but use none.
My tongue and soul in this be hypocrites –
How in my words somever she be shent,
To give them seals never, my soul, consent!

[Exit.]

Scene III

Elsinore. The Castle.

[Enter KING, ROSENCRANTZ, *and* GUILDENSTERN.*]*

King
I like him not; nor stands it safe with us.
To let his madness range. Therefore prepare
    you;
I your commission will forthwith dispatch,
And he to England shall along with you.
The terms of our estate may not endure   5
Hazard so near's as doth hourly grow
Out of his brows.
Guildenstern.
                        We will ourselves provide.
Most holy and religious fear it is
To keep those many many bodies safe
That live and feed upon your Majesty.   10
Rosencrantz
The single and peculiar life is bound
With all the strength and armour of the mind
To keep itself from noyance; but much more
That spirit upon whose weal depends and rests
The lives of many. The cease of majesty   15
Dies not alone, but like a gulf doth draw
What's near it with it. It is a massy wheel,
Fix'd on the summit of the highest mount,
To whose huge spokes ten thousand lesser
    things
Are mortis'd and adjoin'd; which when it falls,   20
Each small annexment, petty consequence,
Attends the boist'rous ruin. Never alone
Did the king sigh, but with a general groan.
King
Arm you, I pray you, to this speedy voyage;
For we will fetters put about this fear,   25
Which now goes too free-footed.

Rosencrantz

We will haste us.

[Exeunt ROSENCRANTZ *and* GUILDENSTERN.*]*

[Enter POLONIUS.*]*

Polonius
My lord, he's going to his mother's closet.
Behind the arras I'll convey myself
To hear the process. I'll warrant she'll tax him
    home;
30   And, as you said, and wisely was it said,
'Tis meet that some more audience than a
    mother,
Since nature makes them partial, should
    o'erhear
The speech, of vantage. Fare you well, my liege.
I'll call upon you ere you go to bed,
And tell you what I know.
King

Thanks, dear my lord.

[Exit POLONIUS.*]*

O, my offence is rank, it smells to heaven;
It hath the primal eldest curse upon't –
A brother's murder! Pray can I not,
Though inclination be as sharp as will.
40   My stronger guilt defeats my strong intent,
And, like a man to double business bound,
I stand in pause where I shall first begin,
And both neglect. What if this cursed hand
Were thicker than itself with brother's blood,
45   Is there not rain enough in the sweet heavens
To wash it white as snow? Whereto serves
    mercy
But to confront the visage of offence?
And what's in prayer but this twofold force,
To be forestalled ere we come to fall,

Or pardon'd being down? Then I'll look up;   50
My fault is past. But, O, what form of prayer
Can serve my turn? 'Forgive me my foul
  murder'!
That cannot be; since I am still possess'd
Of those effects for which I did the murder –
My crown, mine own ambition, and my queen.   55
May one be pardon'd and retain th' offence?
In the corrupted currents of this world
Offence's gilded hand may shove by justice;
And oft 'tis seen the wicked prize itself
Buys out the law. But 'tis not so above: 60
There is no shuffling; there the action lies
In his true nature; and we ourselves compell'd,
Even to the teeth and forehead of our faults,
To give in evidence. What then? What rests?
Try what repentance can. What can it not?   65
Yet what can it when one can not repent?
O wretched state! O bosom black as death!
O limed soul, that, struggling to be free,
Art more engag'd! Help, angels. Make assay:
Bow, stubborn knees; and, heart, with strings of
  steel,   70
Be soft as sinews of the new-born babe.
All may be well.

        [Retires and kneels.]

        [Enter HAMLET.*]*

Hamlet
Now might I do it pat, now 'a is a-praying;
And now I'll do't – and so 'a goes to heaven,
And so am I reveng'd. That would be scann'd: 75
A villain kills my father; and for that,
I, his sole son, do this same villain send
To heaven.
Why, this is hire and salary, not revenge.
'A took my father grossly, full of bread,   80

With all his crimes broad blown, as flush as
  May;
And how his audit stands who knows save
  heaven?
But in our circumstance and course of thought
'Tis heavy with him; and am I then reveng'd
85   To take him in the purging of his soul,
When he is fit and season'd for his passage?
No.
Up, sword, and know thou a more horrid hent.
When he is drunk asleep, or in his rage;
90   Or in th' incestuous pleasure of his bed;
At game, a-swearing, or about some act
That has no relish of salvation in't –
Then trip him, that his heels may kick at
  heaven,
And that his soul may be as damn'd and black
95   As hell, whereto it goes. My mother stays.
This physic but prolongs thy sickly days.

[Exit.]

King [Rising]

My words fly up, my thoughts remain below.
Words without thoughts never to heaven go.

[Exit.]

Scene IV

The Queen's closet.

[Enter QUEEN and POLONIUS.]

Polonius
    'A will come straight. Look you lay home to him;
    Tell him his pranks have been too broad to
      bear with,
    And that your Grace hath screen'd and stood
      between
    Much heat and him. I'll silence me even here.
    Pray you be round with him.
Hamlet [Within]
    Mother, mother, mother!
Queen
    I'll warrant you. Fear me not.
    Withdraw, I hear him coming.

[POLONIUS goes behind the arras.]

[Enter HAMLET.]

Hamlet
    Now, mother, what's the matter?
Queen
    Hamlet, thou hast thy father much offended.
Hamlet
    Mother, you have my father much offended.   10
Queen
    Come, come, you answer with an idle tongue.
Hamlet
    Go, go, you question with a wicked tongue.
Queen
    Why, how now, Hamlet!
Hamlet
                What's the matter now?
Queen
    Have you forgot me?

Hamlet
>   No, by the rood, not so:
You are the Queen, your husband's brother's
15   wife;
And – would it were not so! – you are my
      mother.

Queen
Nay then, I'll set those to you that can speak.

Hamlet
Come, come, and sit you down; you shall not
      budge.
You go not till I set you up a glass
20   Where you may see the inmost part of you.

Queen
What wilt thou do? Thou wilt not murder me?
Help, help, ho!

Polonius [Behind]
What, ho! help, help, help!

Hamlet [Draws]
How now! a rat?
Dead, for a ducat, dead! *[Kills* POLONIUS *with a
      pass through the arras.]*

Polonius [Behind]
O, I am slain!

Queen
O me, what hast thou done?

Hamlet
25   Nay, I know not:
Is it the King?

Queen
O, what a rash and bloody deed is this!

Hamlet
A bloody deed! – almost as bad, good mother,
As kill a king and marry with his brother.

Queen
As kill a king!

Hamlet
30   Ay, lady, it was my word.

[Parting the arras.]

Thou wretched, rash, intruding fool, farewell!
I took thee for thy better. Taken thy fortune;
Thou find'st to be too busy is some danger,
Leave wringing of your hands. Peace; sit you
    down,
And let me wring your heart; for so I shall,   35
If it be made of penetrable stuff;
If damned custom have not braz'd it so
That it be proof and bulwark against sense.

Queen
  What have I done that thou dar'st wag thy
      tongue
  In noise so rude against me?   40

Hamlet
                          Such an act
  That blurs the grace and blush of modesty;
  Calls virtue hypocrite; takes off the rose
  From the fair forehead of an innocent love,
  And sets a blister there; makes marriage-vows
  As false as dicers' oaths. O, such a deed   45
  As from the body of contraction plucks
  The very soul, and sweet religion makes
  A rhapsody of words. Heaven's face does glow
  O'er this solidity and compound mass
  With heated visage, as against the doom –   50
  Is thought-sick at the act.

Queen
                      Ay me, what act,
  That roars so loud and thunders in the index?

Hamlet
  Look here upon this picture and on this.
  The counterfeit presentment of two brothers.
  See what a grace was seated on this brow;   55
  Hyperion's curls; the front of Jove himself;
  An eye like Mars, to threaten and command;
  A station like the herald Mercury
  New lighted on a heaven-kissing hill –

60 A combination and a form indeed
 Where every god did seem to set his seal,
 To give the world assurance of a man.
 This was your husband. Look you now what
  follows:
 Here is your husband, like a mildew'd ear
65 Blasting his wholesome brother. Have you eyes?
 Could you on this fair mountain leave to feed,
 And batten on this moor? Ha! have you eyes?
 You cannot call it love; for at your age
 The heyday in the blood is tame, it's humble,
 And waits upon the judgment; and what
70 judgment
 Would step from this to this? Sense, sure, you
  have,
 Else could you not have motion; but sure that
  sense
 Is apoplex'd; for madness would not err,
 Nor sense to ecstasy was ne'er so thrall'd
75 But it reserv'd some quantity of choice
 To serve in such a difference. What devil was't
 That thus hath cozen'd you at hoodman-
  blind?
 Eyes without feeling, feeling without sight,
 Ears without hands or eyes, smelling sans all,
80 Or but a sickly part of one true sense
 Could not so mope. O shame! where is thy
  blush?
 Rebellious hell,
 If thou canst mutine in a matron's bones,
 To flaming youth let virtue be as wax
85 And melt in her own fire; proclaim no shame
 When the compulsive ardour gives the charge,
 Since frost itself as actively doth burn,
 And reason panders will.
Queen

      O Hamlet, speak no more!
 Thou turn'st my eyes into my very soul;

And there I see such black and grained spots   90
As will not leave their tinct.
Hamlet
                        Nay, but to live
In the rank sweat of an enseamed bed,
Stew'd in corruption, honeying and making
    love
Over the nasty sty!
Queen
               O, speak to me no more!
These words like daggers enter in my ears;   95
No more, sweet Hamlet.
Hamlet
             A murderer and a villain!
A slave that is not twentieth part the tithe
Of your precedent lord; a vice of kings;
A cutpurse of the empire and the rule,
That from a shelf the precious diadem stole   100
And put it in his pocket!
Queen
No more!

[Enter GHOST.]

Hamlet
A king of shreds and patches –
Save me, and hover o'er me with your wings,
You heavenly guards! What would your
    gracious figure?
Queen
Alas, he's mad!   105
Hamlet
Do you not come your tardy son to chide.
That, laps'd in time and passion, lets go by
Th'important acting of your dread command?
O, say!
Ghost
Do not forget; this visitation   110
Is but to whet thy almost blunted purpose.

But look, amazement on thy mother sits.
O, step between her and her fighting soul!
Conceit in weakest bodies strongest works.
115   Speak to her, Hamlet.

Hamlet
How is it with you, lady?

Queen
            Alas, how isn't with you.
That you do bend your eye on vacancy,
And with th' incorporal air do hold discourse?
Forth at your eyes your spirits wildly peep;
And, as the sleeping soldiers in th' alarm,
Your bedded hairs like life in excrements
Start up and stand an end. O gentle son,
Upon the heat and flame of thy distemper
Sprinkle cool patience! Whereon do you look?

Hamlet
125   On him, on him! Look you how pale he glares.
His form and cause conjoin'd, preaching to
    stones,
Would make them capable. – Do not look upon
    me,
Lest with this piteous action you convert
My stern effects; then what I have to do
Will want true colour – tears perchance for
130   blood.

Queen
To whom do you speak this?

Hamlet
Do you see nothing there?

Queen
Nothing at all; yet all that is I see.

Hamlet
Nor did you nothing hear?

Queen
No, nothing but ourselves.

Hamlet
Why, look you there. Look how it steals away.

My father, in his habit as he liv'd!   135
Look where he goes even now out at the portal.

[Exit GHOST.*]*

Queen
    This is the very coinage of your brain.
    This bodiless creation ecstasy
    Is very cunning in.
Hamlet
                Ecstasy!
    My pulse as yours doth temperately keep time,   140
    And makes as healthful music. It is not
      madness
    That I have utt'red. Bring me to the test,
    And I the matter will re-word which madness
    Would gambol from. Mother, for love of grace,
    Lay not that flattering unction to your soul,   145
    That not your trespass but my madness speaks:
    It will but skin and film the ulcerous place,
    Whiles rank corruption, mining all within,
    Infects unseen. Confess yourself to heaven;
    Repent what's past; avoid what is to come;   150
    And do not spread the compost on the weeds,
    To make them ranker. Forgive me this my
      virtue;
    For in the fatness of these pursy times
    Virtue itself of vice must pardon beg,
    Yea, curb and woo for leave to do him good.   155
Queen
    O Hamlet, thou hast cleft my heart in twain.
Hamlet
    O, throw away the worser part of it,
    And live the purer with the other half.
    Good night – but go not to my uncle's bed;
    Assume a virtue, if you have it not.   160
    That monster custom, who all sense doth eat,
    Of habits devil, is angel yet in this,
    That to the use of actions fair and good

He likewise gives a frock or livery
165 That aptly is put on. Refrain to-night;
And that shall lend a kind of easiness
To the next abstinence; the next more easy;
For use almost can change the stamp of nature,
And either curb the devil, or throw him out,
With wondrous potency. Once more, good
170   night;
And when you are desirous to be blest,
I'll blessing beg of you. For this same lord
I do repent; but Heaven hath pleas'd it so,
To punish me with this, and this with me,
175 That I must be their scourge and minister.
I will bestow him, and will answer well
The death I gave him. So, again, good night.
I must be cruel only to be kind;
Thus bad begins and worse remains behind.
One word more, good lady.

Queen
180   What shall I do?

Hamlet
Not this, by no means, that I bid you do:
Let the bloat King tempt you again to bed;
Pinch wanton on your cheek; call you his
      mouse;
And let him, for a pair of reechy kisses,
Or paddling in your neck with his damn'd
185   fingers,
Make you to ravel all this matter out,
That I essentially am not in madness,
But mad in craft. 'Twere good you let him
      know;
For who that's but a queen, fair, sober, wise,
190 Would from a paddock, from a bat, a gib,
Such dear concernings hide? Who would do so?
No, in despite of sense and secrecy,
Unpeg the basket on the house's top,
Let the birds fly, and, like the famous ape,

To try conclusions, in the basket creep   195
And break your own neck down.

Queen

Be thou assur'd, if words be made of breath
And breath of life, I have no life to breathe
What thou hast said to me.

Hamlet

I must to England; you know that?

Queen

                        Alack,   200
I had forgot. 'Tis so concluded on.

Hamlet

There's letters seal'd; and my two
   school-fellows,
Whom I will trust as I will adders fang'd –
They bear the mandate; they must sweep my
   way
And marshal me to knavery. Let it work;   205
For 'tis the sport to have the engineer
Hoist with his own petar; and't shall go hard
But I will delve one yard below their mines
And blow them at the moon. O, 'tis most sweet
When in one line two crafts directly meet.   210
This man shall set me packing.
I'll lug the guts into the neighbour room.
Mother, good night. Indeed, this counsellor
Is now most still, most secret, and most grave,
Who was in life a foolish prating knave.   215
Come, sir, to draw toward an end with you.
Good night, mother.

[Exeunt severally; HAMLET *tugging in* POLONIUS.*]*

ACT FOUR
Scene I

Elsinore. The Castle.

[Enter KING, QUEEN, ROSENCRANTZ, *and*
GUILDENSTERN.*]*

King
There's matter in these sighs, these profound
   heaves,
You must translate; 'tis fit we understand them.
Where is your son?
Queen
Bestow this place on us a little while.

[Exeunt ROSENCRANTZ *and* GUILDENSTERN.*]*

5   Ah, mine own lord, what have I seen to-night!
King
What, Gertrude? How does Hamlet?
Queen
Mad as the sea and wind, when both contend
Which is the mightier. In his lawless fit,
Behind the arras hearing something stir,
10   Whips out his rapier, cries 'A rat, a rat!'
And in this brainish apprehension kills
The unseen good old man.
King
                 O heavy deed!
It had been so with us had we been there.
His liberty is full of threats to all –
15   To you yourself, to us, to every one.
Alas, how shall this bloody deed be answer'd?
It will be laid to us, whose providence
Should have kept short, restrain'd, and out of
   haunt,
This mad young man. But so much was our love,

We would not understand what was most fit;   20
But, like the owner of a foul disease,
To keep it from divulging, let it feed
Even on the pith of life. Where is he gone?

Queen

To draw apart the body he hath kill'd;
O'er whom his very madness, like some ore   25
Among a mineral of metals base,
Shows itself pure: 'a weeps for what is done.

King

O Gertrude, come away!
The sun no sooner shall the mountains touch
But we will ship him hence; and this vile deed   30
We must with all our majesty and skill
Both countenance and excuse. Ho,
    Guildenstern!

[Re-enter ROSENCRANTZ *and* GUILDENSTERN.*]*

Friends, both go join you with some further
    aid:
Hamlet in madness hath Polonius slain,
And from his mother's closet hath he dragg'd
    him;   35
Go seek him out; speak fair, and bring the body
Into the chapel. I pray you haste in this.

[Exeunt ROSENCRANTZ *and* GUILDENSTERN.*]*

Come, Gertrude, we'll call up our wisest friends
And let them know both what we mean to do
And what's untimely done; so haply slander –   40
Whose whisper o'er the world's diameter,
As level as the cannon to his blank,
Transports his pois'ned shot – may miss our
    name,
And hit the woundless air. O, come away!
My soul is full of discord and dismay.   45

[Exeunt.]

Scene II

Elsinore. The Castle.

[Enter HAMLET.*]*

Hamlet
  Safely stow'd.
Gentlemen [Within]
  Hamlet! Lord Hamlet!
Hamlet
  But soft! What noise? Who calls on Hamlet? O,
  here they come!

  [Enter ROSENCRANTZ *and* GUILDENSTERN.*]*

Rosencrantz
  What have you done, my lord, with the dead
5   body?
Hamlet
  Compounded it with dust, whereto 'tis kin.
Rosencrantz
  Tell us where 'tis, that we may take it thence
  And bear it to the chapel.
Hamlet
  Do not believe it.
Rosencrantz
10   Believe what?
Hamlet
  That I can keep your counsel, and not mine own.
  Besides, to be demanded of a sponge – what repli-
13   cation should be made by the son of a king?
Rosencrantz
  Take you me for a sponge, my lord?
Hamlet
  Ay, sir; that soaks up the King's countenance, his
  rewards, his authorities. But such officers do the
  King best service in the end: he keeps them, like
  an ape an apple in the corner of his jaw; first
  mouth'd, to be last swallowed; when he needs

what you have glean'd, it is but squeezing you
and, sponge, you shall be dry again.   20

Rosencrantz
    I understand you not, my lord.

Hamlet
    I am glad of it; a knavish speech sleeps in a foolish
    ear.

Rosencrantz
    My lord, you must tell us where the body is, and
    go with us to the King.   25

Hamlet
    The body is with the King, but the King is not
    with the body. The King is a thing –

Guildenstern
    A thing, my lord!

Hamlet
    Of nothing. Bring me to him.
    Hide fox, and all after.   30

                    [Exeunt.]

Scene III

Elsinore. The Castle.

[Enter KING, *attended.]*

King
    I have sent to seek him, and to find the body.
    How dangerous is it that this man goes loose!
    Yet must not we put the strong law on him:
    He's lov'd of the distracted multitude,
5   Who like not in their judgement but their eyes;
    And where 'tis so, th' offender's scourge is weigh'd,
    But never the offence. To bear all smooth and even,
    This sudden sending him away must seem
    Deliberate pause. Diseases desperate grown
10   By desperate appliance are reliev'd,
    Or not at all.

[Enter ROSENCRANTZ.*]*

                How now! what hath befall'n?

Rosencrantz
    Where the dead body is bestow'd, my lord,
    We cannot get from him.

King
                    But where is he?

Rosencrantz
    Without, my lord; guarded, to know your pleasure.

King
15   Bring him before us.

Rosencrantz
    Ho. Guildenstern! bring in the lord.

[Enter HAMLET *and* GUILDENSTERN.*]*

King
    Now, Hamlet, where's Polonius?

Hamlet
At supper.
King
At supper! Where?   19
Hamlet
Not where he eats, but where 'a is eaten: a certain
convocation of politic worms are e'en at him.
Your worm is your only emperor for diet: we fat
all creatures else to fat us, and we fat ourselves
for maggots; your fat king and your lean beggar
is but variable service – two dishes. but to one
table. That's the end.   25
King
Alas, alas!
Hamlet
A man may fish with the worm that hath eat of
a king, and eat of the fish that hath fed of that
worm.
King
What dost thou mean by this?
Hamlet
Nothing but to show you how a king may go a   31
progress through the guts of a beggar.   32
King
Where is Polonius?
Hamlet
In heaven; send thither to see; if your messenger
find him not there, seek him i' th' other place
yourself. But if, indeed, you find him not within
this month, you shall nose him as you go up the
stairs into the lobby.   37
King [To ATTENDANTS]
Go seek him there.
Hamlet
'A will stay till you come.

[Exeunt ATTENDANTS.*]*

King

40   Hamlet, this deed, for thine especial safety –
        Which we do tender, as we dearly grieve
        For that which thou hast done – must send
            thee hence
        With fiery quickness. Therefore prepare thyself;
        The bark is ready, and the wind at help,
45   Th' associates tend, and everything is bent
        For England.

Hamlet

                        For England!

King

                                Ay, Hamlet.

Hamlet

                                        Good!

King

        So is it, if thou knew'st our purposes.

Hamlet

        I see a cherub that sees them.
        But, come; for England! Farewell, dear mother.

King

50   Thy loving father, Hamlet.

Hamlet

        My mother: father and mother is man and wife;
        man and wife is one flesh; and so, my mother.
        Come, for England.

                        [Exit.]

King

        Follow him at foot; tempt him with speed
            aboard;
55   Delay it not; I'll have him hence to-night.
        Away! for everything is seal'd and done
        That else leans on th' affair. Pray you make
            haste.   *[Exeunt all but the* KING.]
        And, England, if my love thou hold'st at aught –
        As my great power thereof may give thee sense,
60   Since yet thy cicatrice looks raw and red

After the Danish sword, and thy free awe
Pays homage to us – thou mayst not coldly set
Our sovereign process; which imports at full,
By letters congruing to that effect,
The present death of Hamlet. Do it, England: 65
For like the hectic in my blood he rages,
And thou must cure me. Till I know 'tis done,
Howe'er my haps, my joys were ne'er begun.

[Exit.]

Scene IV

A plain in Denmark.

[Enter FORTINBRAS *with his Army over the stage.]*

Fortinbras
Go, Captain, from me greet the Danish king.
Tell him that by his licence Fortinbras
Craves the conveyance of a promis'd march
Over his kingdom. You know the rendezvous.
If that his Majesty would aught with us,
We shall express our duty in his eye;
5   And let him know so.
Captain
                                    I will do't, my lord.
Fortinbras
Go softly on.

[Exeunt all but the Captain.]

[Enter HAMLET, ROSENCRANTZ, GUILDENSTERN, *and Others.]*

Hamlet
Good sir, whose powers are these?
Captain
They are of Norway, sir.
Hamlet
10   How purpos'd, sir, I pray you?
Captain
Against some part of Poland.
Hamlet
Who commands them, sir?
Captain
The nephew to old Norway, Fortinbras.
Hamlet
15   Goes it against the main of Poland, sir,
Or for some frontier?

Captain
    Truly to speak, and with no addition,
    We go to gain a little patch of ground
    That hath in it no profit but the name.
    To pay five ducats, five, I would not farm it;   20
    Nor will it yield to Norway or the Pole
    A ranker rate should it be sold in fee.
Hamlet
    Why, then the Polack never will defend it.
Captain
    Yes, it is already garrison'd.
Hamlet
    Two thousand souls and twenty thousand
      ducats   25
    Will not debate the question of this straw.
    This is th' imposthume of much wealth and
      peace,
    That inward breaks, and shows no cause
      without
    Why the man dies. I humbly thank you, sir.   29
Captain
    God buy you, sir. *[Exit.]*
Rosencrantz
                    Will't please you go, my lord?   30
Hamlet
    I'll be with you straight. Go a little before.

        [Exeunt all but HAMLET.]

    How all occasions do inform against me,
    And spur my dull revenge! What is a man,
    If his chief good and market of his time
    Be but to sleep and feed? A beast, no more!   35
    Sure he that made us with such large discourse,
    Looking before and after, gave us not
    That capability and godlike reason
    To fust in us unus'd. Now, whether it be
    Bestial oblivion, or some craven scruple   40
    Of thinking too precisely on th' event –

A thought which, quarter'd, hath but one part
   wisdom
And ever three parts coward – I do not know
Why yet I live to say 'This thing's to do',
Sith I have cause, and will, and strength, and
45   means,
To do't. Examples gross as earth exhort me:
Witness this army, of such mass and charge,
Led by a delicate and tender prince,
Whose spirit, with divine ambition puff'd,
50   Makes mouths at the invisible event,
Exposing what is mortal and unsure
To all that fortune, death, and danger, dare,
Even for an egg-shell. Rightly to be great
Is not to stir without great argument,
But greatly to find quarrel in a straw,
When honour's at the stake. How stand I, then,
That have a father kill'd, a mother stain'd,
Excitements of my reason and my blood,
And let all sleep, while to my shame I see
60   The imminent death of twenty thousand men
That, for a fantasy and trick of fame,
Go to their graves like beds, fight for a plot
Whereon the numbers cannot try the cause,
Which is not tomb enough and continent
To hide the slain? O, from this time forth,
My thoughts be bloody, or be nothing worth!

[*Exit.*]

Scene V

Elsinore. The Castle.

[*Enter* QUEEN, HORATIO, *and a* GENTLEMAN.]

Queen
I will not speak with her.

Gentleman
She is importunate, indeed distract.
Her mood will needs be pitied.

Queen
                    What would she have?

Gentleman
She speaks much of her father, says she hears
There's tricks i'th' world, and hems, and beats
    her heart;   5
Spurns enviously at straws; speaks things in
    doubt,
That carry but half sense. Her speech is
    nothing,
Yet the unshaped use of it doth move
The hearers to collection; they yawn at it,
And botch the words up fit to their own
    thoughts;   10
Which, as her winks and nods and gestures
    yields them,
Indeed would make one think there might be
    thought,
Though nothing sure, yet much unhappily.

Horatio
'Twere good she were spoken with; for she may
    strew
Dangerous conjectures in ill-breeding minds.   15

Queen
Let her come in. [*Exit* GENTLEMAN.]
[*Aside*] To my sick soul, as sin's true nature is,
Each toy seems prologue to some great amiss.
So full of artless jealousy is guilt,

20   It spills itself in fearing to be spilt.

[Enter OPHELIA *distracted.]*

Ophelia
    Where is the beautous Majesty of Denmark?
Queen
    How now, Ophelia!
Ophelia [Sings]

        How should I your true love know
            From another one?
25   By his cockle hat and staff,
            And his sandal shoon.

Queen
    Alas, sweet lady, what imports this song?
Ophelia
    Say you? Nay, pray you mark.
    [Sings] He is dead and gone, lady,
30   He is dead and gone;
            At his head a grass-green turf,
            At his heels a stone.
            O, ho!
Queen
                Nay, but, Ophelia –
Ophelia
                    Pray you mark.
    [Sings] White his shroud as the mountain snow –

[Enter KING.*]*

Queen
35   Alas, look here, my lord.
Ophelia
    Larded with sweet flowers;
    Which bewept to the grave did not go
    With true-love showers.
King
39   How do you, pretty lady?

Ophelia
> Well, God dild you! They say the owl was a baker's
> daughter. Lord, we know what we are, but know
> not what we may be. God be at your table!

King
> Conceit upon her father.

Ophelia
> Pray let's have no words of this; but when they
> ask you what it means, say you this: 45

> *[Sings]* To-morrow is Saint Valentine's day,
> >   All in the morning betime,
> > And I a maid at your window,
> >   To be your Valentine.

> Then up he rose, and donn'd his clothes,   50
> And dupp'd the chamber-door;
> Let in the maid, that out a maid
> Never departed more.

King
> Pretty Ophelia!

Ophelia
> Indeed, la, without an oath, I'll make an end on't.   55

> *[Sings]* By Gis and by Saint Charity,
> >   Alack, and fie for shame!
> > Young men will do't, if they come to't;
> >   By Cock, they are to blame.
> > Quoth she 'Before you tumbled me,   60
> >   You promis'd me to wed'.

> He answers:
> 'So would I 'a done, by yonder sun,
> An thou hadst not come to my bed'.

King
> How long hath she been thus?   65

Ophelia
> I hope all will be well. We must be patient; but
> I cannot choose but weep to think they would
> lay him i' th' cold ground. My brother shall know

of it' and so I thank you for your good counsel.
Come, my coach! Good night, ladies; good night,
sweet ladies, good night, good night.

[Exit.]

King
Follow her close; give her good watch, I pray you.

[Exeunt HORATIO *and* GENTLEMAN.*]*

O, this is the poison of deep grief; it springs
All from her father's death. And now behold –
O Gertrude, Gertrude!
When sorrows come, they come not single
75   spies,
But in battalions! First, her father slain;
Next, your son gone, and he most violent
      author
Of his own just remove; the people muddied,
Thick and unwholesome in their thoughts and
      whispers
For good Polonius' death; and we have done
80   but greenly
In hugger-mugger to inter him; poor Ophelia
Divided from herself and her fair judgment,
Without the which we are pictures, or mere
      beasts;
Last, and as much containing as all these,
85   Her brother is in secret come from France;
Feeds on his wonder, keeps himself in clouds,
And wants not buzzers to infect his ear
With pestilent speeches of his father's death;
Wherein necessity, of matter beggar'd,
90   Will nothing stick our person to arraign
In ear and ear. O my dear Gertrude, this,
Like to a murd'ring piece, in many places
Gives me superfluous death.

[A noise within.]

Queen
　Alack, what noise is this?
King
　Attend!

　　　　[Enter a GENTLEMAN.*]*

　Where are my Switzers? Let them guard the
　　　door.
　What is the matter?
Gentleman
　　　　　　　　Save yourself, my lord:　　　　95
　The ocean, overpeering of his list,
　Eats not the flats with more impitious haste
　Than young Laertes, in a riotous head,
　O'erbears your officers. The rabble call him lord;
　And, as the world were now but to begin,　　　100
　Antiquity forgot, custom not known.
　The ratifiers and props of every word,
　The cry 'Choose we; Laertes shall be king'.
　Caps, hands, and tongues, applaud it to the
　　　clouds,
　'Laertes shall be king, Laertes king'.　　　　105
Queen
　How cheerfully on the false trail they cry!

　　　　[Noise within.]

　O, this is counter, you false Danish dogs!
King
　The doors are broke.

　　　[Enter LAERTES, *with Others, in arms.]*

Laertes
　Where is this king? – Sirs, stand you all
　　　without.
All
　No, let's come in.
Laertes
　　　　　　　　I pray you give me leave.　　　110

All
We will, we will.

[Exeunt.]

Laertes
I thank you. Keep the door. – O thou vile king,
Give me my father!

Queen
                Calmly, good Laertes.

Laertes
That drop of blood that's calm proclaims me
    bastard;
115   Cries cuckold to my father; brands the harlot
Even here, between the chaste unsmirched
    brow
Of my true mother.

King
                What is the cause, Laertes,
That thy rebellion looks so giant-like?
Let him go, Gertrude; do not fear our person:
120   There's such divinity doth hedge a king
That reason can but peep to what it would,
Acts little of his will. Tell me, Laertes,
Why thou art thus incens'd. Let him go,
    Gertrude.
Speak, man.

Laertes
Where is my father?

King
                Dead.

Queen
125   But not by him.

King
Let him demand his fill.

Laertes
How came he dead? I'll not be juggled with.
To hell, allegiance! Vows, to the blackest devil!
Conscience and grace, to the profoundest pit!

I dare damnation. To this point I stand,   130
That both the worlds I give to negligence,
Let come what comes; only I'll be reveng'd
Most throughly for my father.

King

Who shall stay you?

Laertes

          My will, not all the world's.
And for my means, I'll husband them so well   135
They shall go far with little.

King

             Good Laertes,
If you desire to know the certainly
Of dear father, is't writ in your revenge
That, swoopstake, you will draw both friend
   and foe,
Winner and loser?

Laertes

          None but his enemies.   140

King

Will you know them, then?

Laertes

To his good friends thus wide I'll ope my arms
And, like the kind life-rend'ring pelican,
Repast them with my blood.

King

          Why, now you speak
Like a good child and a true gentleman.   145
That I am guiltless of your father's death,
And am most sensibly in grief for it,
It shall as level to your judgement 'pear
As day does to your eye.

[A noise within: 'Let her come in.']

Laertes

How now! What noise is that?   150

[Re-enter OPHELIA.]

O, heat dry up my brains! tears seven times salt
Burn out the sense and virtue of mine eye!
By heaven, thy madness shall be paid with
    weight
Till our scale turn the beam. O rose of May!
155   Dear maid, kind sister, sweet Ophelia!
O heavens! is't possible a young maid's wits
Should be as mortal as an old man's life?
Nature is fine in love; and where 'tis fine
It sends some precious instance of itself
160   After the thing it loves.
Ophelia [Sings]

    They bore him barefac'd on the bier;
     Hey non nonny, nonny, hey nonny;
    And in his grave rain'd many a tear –

Fare you well, my dove!
Laertes
    Hadst thou thy wits, and didst persuade
165   revenge,
    It could not move thus.
Ophelia
    You must sing 'A-down, a-down', an you call him
    a-down-a. O, how the wheel becomes it! It is the
    false steward, that stole his master's daughter.
Laertes
170   This nothing's more than matter.
Ophelia
    There's rosemary, that's for remembrance; pray
    you, love, remember. And there is pansies, that's
    for thoughts.
Laertes
    A document in madness – thoughts and remem-
174   brance fitted.
Ophelia
    There's fennel for you, and columbines.
    There's rue for you; and here's some for me. We
    may call it herb of grace a Sundays. O, you must

wear your rue with a difference. There's a daisy.
I would give you some violets, but they wither'd
all when my father died. They say 'a made a good
end.   182
[Sings] For bonny sweet Robin is all my joy.
Laerthes
    Thought and affliction, passion, hell itself,
    She turns to favour and to prettiness.   185
Ophelia *[Sings]*

        And will 'a not come again?
        And will 'a not come again?
            No, no, he is dead,
            Go to thy death-bed,
        He never will come again.   190
        His beard was as white as snow,
        All flaxen was his poll;
            He is gone, he is gone,
            And we cast away moan:
        God-a-mercy on his soul!   195

    And of all Christian souls, I pray God. God buy
      you.

[Exit.]

Laertes
    Do you see this, O God?
King
    Laertes, I must commune with your grief,
    Or you deny me right. Go but apart,
    Make choice of whom your wisest friends you
      will,   200
    And they shall hear and judge 'twixt you and
      me.
    If by direct or by collateral hand
    They find us touch'd, we will our kingdom
      give,
    Our crown, our life, and all that we call ours,
    To you in satisfaction; but if not,   205

Be you content to lend your patience to us,
And we shall jointly labour with your soul
To give it due content.

Laertes
                              Let this be so.
His means of death, his obscure funeral –
210   No, trophy, sword, nor hatchment, o'er his
            bones,
No noble rite nor formal ostentation –
Cry to be heard, as 'twere from heaven to
            earth,
That I must call't in question.

King
                              So you shall;
And where th' offence is, let the great axe fall.
215   I pray you go with me.

                    [Exeunt.]

Scene VI

Elsinore. The Castle.

[Enter HORATIO *with an* ATTENDANT.*]*

Horatio
What are they that would speak with me?
Attendant
Sea-faring men, sir; they say they have letters for
you.
Horatio
Let them come in.

[Exit ATTENDANT.*]*

I do not know from what part of the world
I should be greeted, if not from Lord Hamlet.   5

[Enter SAILORS.*]*

Sailor
God bless you, sir.
Horatio
Let Him bless thee too.
Sailor
'A shall, sir, an't please Him. There's a letter for
you, sir, it came from th' ambassador that was
bound for England – if your name be Horatio, as
I am let to know it is.   11
Horatio [Reads]
'Horatio, when thou shalt have overlook'd this,
give these fellows some means to the King: they
have letters for him. Ere we were two days old at
sea, a pirate of very warlike appointment gave us
chase. Finding ourselves too slow of sail, we put
on a compelled valour; and in the grapple I
boarded them. On the instant they got clear of
our ship; so I alone became their prisoner. They
have dealt with me like thieves of mercy; but they
knew what they did: I am to do a good turn for

them. Let the King have the letters I have sent;
and repair thou to me with as much speed as
thou wouldest fly death. I have words to speak
in thine ear will make thee dumb; yet are they
much too light for the bore of the matter. These
good fellows will bring thee where I am.
Rosencrantz and Guildenstern hold their course
for England; of them I have much to tell thee.
Farewell.
He that thou knowest thine, HAMLET.'
Come, I will give you way for these your
  letters,
And do't the speedier that you may direct me
To him from whom you brought them.

[Exeunt.]

Scene VII

Elsinore. The Castle.

[Enter KING *and* LAERTES.*]*

King
   Now must your conscience my acquittance seal,
   And you must put me in your heart for friend,
   Sith you have heard, and with a knowing ear,
   That he which hath your noble father slain
   Pursu'd my life.

Laertes
               It well appears. But tell me   5
   Why you proceeded not against these feats,
   So crimeful and so capital in nature,
   As by your safety, wisdom, all things else,
   You mainly were stirr'd up.

King
                O, for two special reasons,
   Which may to you, perhaps, seem much
      unsinew'd,   10
   But yet to me th'are strong. The Queen his
      mother
   Lives almost by his looks; and for myself,
   My virtue or my plague, be it either which –
   She is so conjunctive to my life and soul
   That, as the star moves not but in his sphere,   15
   I could not but by her. The other motive,
   Why to a public count I might not go,
   Is the great love the general gender bear him;
   Who, dipping all his faults in their affection,
   Work like the spring that turneth wood to stone,   20
   Convert his gyves to graces; so that my arrows,
   Too slightly timber'd for so loud a wind,
   Would have reverted to my bow again.
   But not where I have aim'd them.

Laertes
   And so have I a noble father lost;   25

A sister driven into desp'rate terms,
Whose worth, if praises may go back again,
Stood challenger on mount of all the age
For her perfections. But my revenge will come.

King
Break not your sleeps for that. You must not
30   think
That we are made of stuff so flat and dull
That we can let our beard be shook with
      danger,
And think it pastime. You shortly shall hear
      more.
I lov'd your father, and we love our self;
35   And that, I hope, will teach you to imagine –

[Enter a MESSENGER *with letters.]*

How now! What news?
Messenger
Letters, my lord, from Hamlet:
These to your Majesty; this to the Queen.
King
From Hamlet! Who brought them?
Messenger
Sailors, my lord, they say; I saw them not.
They were given me by Claudio; he receiv'd
40   them
Of him that brought them.
King
Laertes, you shall hear them.
Leave us.

[Exit MESSENGER.*]*

[Reads] 'High and Mighty. You shall know I am
set naked on your kingdom. To-morrow shall I
beg leave to see your kingly eyes; when I shall,
first asking your pardon thereunto, recount the
occasion of my sudden and more strange return.
HAMLET.'

What should this mean? Are all the rest come
    back? 48
Or is it some abuse, and no such thing?

Laertes

Know you the hand? 50

King

'Tis Hamlet's character. 'Naked'!
And in a postscript here, he says 'alone'.
Can you devise me?

Laertes

I am lost in it, my lord. But let him come;
It warms the very sickness in my heart 55
That I shall live and tell him to his teeth
'Thus didest thou'.

King

            If it be so, Laertes –
As how should it be so, how otherwise? –
Will you be rul'd by me?

Laertes

            Ay, my lord;
So you will not o'errule me to a peace. 60

King

To thine own peace. If he be now return'd,
As checking at his voyage, and that he means
No more to undertake it, I will work him
To an exploit now ripe in my device,
Under the which he shall not choose but fall; 65
And for his death, no wind of blame shall
    breathe;
But even his mother shall uncharge the practice
And call it accident.

Laertes

          My lord, I will be rul'd
The rather, if you could devise it so
That I might be the organ.

King

          It falls right. 70
You have been talk'd of since your travel much,

And that in Hamlet's hearing, for a quality
Wherein they say you shine. Your sum of parts
Did not together pluck such envy from him
75   As did that one; and that, in my regard,
Of the unworthiest siege.

Laertes

                    What part is that, my lord?

King

A very riband in the cap of youth,
Yet needful too; for youth no less becomes
The light and careless livery that it wears
80   Than settled age his sables and his weeds,
Importing health and graveness. Two months
    since
Here was a gentleman of Normandy –
I have seen myself, and serv'd against, the
    French,
And they can well on horseback; but this
    gallant
85   Had witchcraft in't; he grew unto his seat,
And to such wondrous doing brought his
    horse,
As had he been incorps'd and demi-natur'd
With the brave beast. So far he topp'd my
    thought,
That I, in forgery of shapes and tricks,
Come short of what he did.

Laertes

90   A Norman wasn't?

King

A Norman.

Laertes

Upon my life, Lamord.

King

                            The very same.

Laertes

I know him well. He is the brooch indeed
And gem of all the nation.

King
He made confession of you;   95
And gave you such a masterly report
For art and exercise in your defence,
And for your rapier most especial,
That he cried out 'twould be a sight indeed
If one could match you. The scrimers of their
    nation   100
He swore had neither motion, guard, nor eye,
If you oppos'd them. Sir, this report of his
Did Hamlet so envenom with his envy
That he could nothing do but wish and beg
Your sudden coming o'er, to play with you.   105
Now, out of this –

Laertes
                    What out of this, my lord?

King
Laertes, was your father dear to you?
Or are you like the painting of a sorrow,
A face without a heart?

Laertes
                    Why ask you this?

King
Not that I think you did not love your father;   110
But that I know love is begun by time,
And that I see, in passages of proof,
Time qualifies the spark and fire of it.
There lives within the very flame of love
A kind of wick or snuff that will abate it;   115
And nothing is at a like goodness still;
For goodness, growing to a pleurisy,
Dies in his own too much. That we would do,
We should do when we would; for this 'would'
    changes,
And hath abatements and delays as many   120
As there are tongues, are hands, are accidents;
And then this 'should' is like a spend-thirft's
    sigh

That hurts by easing. But to the quick of th'
    ulcer:
Hamlet comes back; what would you undertake
125   To show yourself in deed your father's son
More than in words?

Laertes

                    To cut his throat i' th' church.

King

No place, indeed, should murder sanctuarize;
Revenge should have no bounds. But, good
    Laertes,
Will you do this? Keep close within your
    chamber.
Hamlet return'd shall know you are come
130   home.
We'll put on those shall praise your excellence,
And set a double varnish on the fame
The Frenchman gave you; bring you, in fine,
    together,
And wager on your heads. He, being remiss,
135   Most generous, and free from all contriving,
Will not peruse the foils; so that with ease
Or with a little shuffling, you may choose
A sword unbated, and, in a pass of practice,
Requite him for your father.

Laertes

                       I will do't;
140   And for that purpose I'll anoint my sword.
I bought an unction of a mountebank,
So mortal that but dip a knife in it,
Where it draws blood no cataplasm so rare,
Collected from all simples that have virtue
Under the moon, can save the thing from
145   death
That is but scratch'd withal. I'll touch my point
With this contagion, that. if I gall him slightly,
It may be death.

King

Let's further think of this;
Weigh what convenience both of time and means
May fit us to our shape. If this should fail,   150
And that our drift look through our bad
  performance.
'Twere better not assay'd, therefore this project
Should have a back or second, that might hold
If this did blast in proof. Soft! let me see.
We'll make a solemn wager on your cunnings –   155
  I ha't.
When in your motion you are hot and dry –
As make your bouts more violent to that end –
And that he calls for drink, I'll have preferr'd
  him
A chalice for the nonce; whereon but sipping,   160
If he by chance escape your venom'd stuck,
Our purpose may hold there. But stay; what
  noise?

[Enter QUEEN.*]*

Queen
One woe doth tread upon another's heel,
So fast they follow. Your sister's drown'd,
Laertes.   165
Laertes
Drown'd! O, where?
Queen
There is a willow grows aslant the brook
That shows his hoar leaves in the glassy stream;
Therewith fantastic garlands did she make
Of crowflowers, nettles, daisies, and long
  purples   170
That liberal shepherds give a grosser name,
But our cold maids do dead men's fingers call
  them.
There, on the pendent boughs her coronet
  weeds
Clamb'ring to hang, an envious silver broke;

175   When down her weedy trophies and herself
        Fell in the weeping brook. Her clothes spread
          wide
        And, mermaid-like, awhile they bore her up;
        Which time she chanted snatches of old lauds,
        As one incapable of her own distress,
180   Or like a creature native and indued
        Unto that element; but long it could not be
        Till that her garments, heavy with their drink,
        Pull'd the poor wretch from her melodious lay
        To muddy death.

Laertes
                    Alas, then she is drown'd!

Queen
185   Drown'd, drown'd.

Laertes
        Too much of water hast thou, poor Ophelia,
        And therefore I forbid my tears; but yet
        It is our trick; nature her custom holds,
        Let shame say what it will. When these are
          gone,
190   The woman will be out. Adieu, my lord.
        I have a speech o' fire that fain would blaze
        But that this folly douts it.

                [Exit.]

King
                    Let's follow, Gertrude.
        How much I had to do to calm his rage!
        Now fear I this will give it start again;
195   Therefore let's follow.

                [Exeunt.]

ACT FIVE
Scene I

Elsinore. A churchyard.

[Enter two CLOWNS *with spades and picks.]*

1 Clown
Is she to be buried in Christian burial when she
willfully seeks her own salvation?

2 Clown
I tell thee she is; therefore make her grave straight.
The crowner hath sat on her, and finds it Christian
burial.   5

1 Clown
How can that be, unless she drown'd herself in
her own defence?

2 Clown
Why, 'tis found so.

1 Clown
It must be 'see offendendo'; it cannot be else. For
here lies the point: if I drown myself wittingly, it
argues an act; and an act hath three branches – it
is to act, to do, to perform; argal, she drown'd
herself wittingly.   13

2 Clown
Nay, but hear you, Goodman Delver.

1 Clown
Give me leave. Here lies the water; good. Here
stands the man; good. If the man go to this water
and drown himself, it is, will he, nill he, he goes
– mark you that; but if the water come to him
and drown him, he drowns not himself. Argal,
he that is not guilty of his own death shortens
not his own life.

2 Clown
But is this law?   21

1 Clown
Ay, marry, is't; crowner's quest law.

2 Clown
Will you ha the truth an't? If this had not been
a gentlewoman, she should have been buried out
25 a Christian burial.

1 Clown
Why, there thou say'st; and the more pity that
great folk should have count'nance in this world
to drown or hang themselves more than their
even Christen. Come, my spade. There is not
ancient gentlemen but gard'ners, ditchers, and
31 grave-makers; they hold up Adam's profession.

2 Clown
Was he a gentleman?

1 Clown
'A was the first that ever bore arms.

2 Clown
34 Why, he had none.

1 Clown
What, art a heathen? How dost thou understand
the Scripture? The Scripture says Adam digg'd.
Could he dig without arms? I'll put another question to thee. If thou answerest me not to the
purpose, confess thyself –

2 Clown
40 Go to.

1 Clown
What is he that builds stronger than either the
mason, the shipwright, or the carpenter?

2 Clown
The gallows-maker; for that frame outlives a
44 thousand tenants.

1 Clown
I like thy wit well; in good faith the gallows
does well; but how does it well? It does well to
those that do ill. Now thou dost ill to say the
gallows is built stronger than the church; argal,

the gallows may do well to thee. To 't again, come. 49

2 Clown
Who builds stronger than a mason, a shipwright, or a carpenter?

1 Clown
Ay, tell me that, and unyoke.

2 Clown
Marry, now I can tell.

1 Clown
To 't.

2 Clown
Mass, I cannot tell. 55

[Enter HAMLET *and* HORATIO, *after off.]*

1 Clown
Cudgel thy brains no more about it, for your dull ass will not mend his pace with beating; and when you are ask'd this question next, say 'a grave-maker': the houses he makes lasts till doomsday. Go, get thee to Yaughan; fetch me a stoup of liquor. 60

[Exit SECOND CLOWN.*]*

[Digs and sings] In youth, when I did love, did love,
  Methought it was very sweet,
To contract-o-the time for-a my behove,
O, methought there-a-was nothing-a meet.

Hamlet
Has this fellow no feeling of his business, that 'a sings in grave-making? 66

Horatio
Custom hath made it in him a property of easiness.

Hamlet
'Tis e'en so; the hand of little employment hath the daintier sense. 70

1 Clown [Sings]
　　But age, with his stealing steps,
　　Hath clawed me in his clutch,
　　And hath shipped me intil the land,
74　　As if I had never been such.

　　　　　[Thrown up a skull.]

Hamlet
　　That skill had a tongue in it, and could sing once.
　　How the knave jowls it to the ground, as if 'twere
　　Cain's jawbone, that did the first murder! This
　　might be the pate of a politician, which this ass
　　now o'erreaches; one that would circumvent God,
80　　might it not?
Horatio
　　It might, my lord.
Hamlet
　　Or of a courtier; which could say 'Good morrow,
　　sweet lord! How dost thou, sweet lord?' This might
　　be my Lord Such-a-one, that praised my Lord
　　Such-a-one's horse, when 'a meant to beg it –
　　might it not?
Horatio
85　　Ay, my lord.
Hamlet
　　When, e'en so; and now my Lady
　　Worm's, chapless, and knock'd about the mazard
　　with a sexton's spade. Here's fine revolution, an
　　we had the trick to see't. Did these bones cost no
　　more the breeding but to play at loggats with
90　　them? Mine ache to think on't.
1 Clown [Sings]

　　　　A pick-axe and a spade, a spade,
　　　　　For and a shrouding sheet:
　　　　O, a pit of clay for to be made
　　　　　For such a guest is meet.

　　　　　[Throws up another skull.]

Hamlet
There's another. Why may not that be the skull of a lawyer? Where be his quiddities now, his quillets, his cases, his tenures, and his tricks? Why does he suffer this rude knave now to knock him about the sconce with a dirty shovel, and will not tell him of his action of battery? Hum! This fellow might be in's time a great buyer of land, with his statutes, his recognizances, his fines, his double vouchers, his recoveries. Is this the fine of his fines, and the recovery of his recoveries, to have his fine pate full of fine dirt? Will his vouchers vouch him no more of his purchases, and double ones too, than the length and breadth of a pair of indentures? The very conveyances of his lands will scarcely lie in this box; and must th' inheritor himself have no more, ha?

Horatio
Not a job more, my lord.

Hamlet
Is not parchment made of sheep-skins?   110

Horatio
Ay, my lord, and of claves' skins too.

Hamlet
They are sheep and calves which seek out assurance in that. I will speak to this fellow.
Whose grave's this, sirrah?

1 Clown
Mine, sir. *[Sings]*   115

    O, a pit of clay for to be made
    For such a guest is meet.

Hamlet
I think it be think indeed, for thou liest in't.

1 Clown
You lie out on't, sir, and therefore 'tis not yours.
For my part, I do not lie in't, yet it is mine.   120

Hamlet
Thou dost lie in't, to be in't and say it is thine; 'tis
for the dead, not for the quick; therefore thou liest.

1 Clown
'Tis a quick lie, sir, 'twill away again from me to
you.

Hamlet
125   What man dost thou dig it for?

1 Clown
For no man, sir.

Hamlet
What woman, then?

1 Clown
For none neither.

Hamlet
Who is to be buried in't?

1 Clown
130   One that was a woman, sir; but, rest her soul,
she's dead.

Hamlet
How absolute the knave is! We must speak by the
card, or equivocation will undo us.
By the Lord, Horatio, this three years I have took
note of it: the age is grown so picked that the toe
of the peasant comes so near the heel of the
courtier, he galls his kibe. How long hast thou
been a grave-maker?

1 Clown
Of all the days i' th' year, I came to't that day
140   that our last King Hamlet overcame Fortinbras.

Hamlet
How long is that since?

I Clown
Cannot you tell that? Every fool can tell that: it
was that very day that young Hamlet was born
– he that is mad, and sent into England.

Hamlet
145   Ay, marry, why was he sent into England?

1 Clown
   Why, because 'a was mad: 'a shall recover his wits
   there; or, if 'a do not, 'tis no great matter there.
Hamlet
   Why?
1 Clown
   'Twill not be seen in him there: there the men
   are as mad as he.   150
Hamlet
   How came he mad?
1 Clown
   Very strangely, they say.
Hamlet
   How strangely?
1 Clown
   Faith, e'en with losing his wits.
Hamlet
   Upon what ground?   155
1 Clown
   Why, here in Denmark. I have been sexton here,
   man and boy, thirty years.
Hamlet
   How long will a man lie i' th' earth ere he rot?
1 Clown
   Faith, if 'a be not rotten before 'a die – as we have
   many pocky corses now-a-days that will scarce
   hold the laying in – 'a will last you some eight
   year or nine year. A tanner will last you nine year. 162
Hamlet
   Why he more than another?
1 Clown
   Why, sir, his hide is so tann'd with his trade that
   'a will keep out water a great while; and your
   water is a sore decayer of your whoreson dead
   body. Here's a skull now; this skull has lien you
   i' th' earth three and twenty years.
Hamlet
   Whose was it?   170

1 Clown

A whoreson mad fellow's it was. Whose do you think it was?

Hamlet

Nay, I know not.

1 Clown

A pestilence on him for a mad rogue!

'A poured a flagon of Rhenish on my head once. This same skull, sir, was, sir, Yorick's skull, the

176 King's jester.

Hamlet

This?

1 Clown

E'en that.

Hamlet

Let me see. *[Takes the skull]* Alas, poor Yorick! I knew him, Horatio: a fellow of infinite jest, of most excellent fancy; he hath borne me on his back a thousand times. And now how abhorred in my imagination it is! My gorge rises at it. Here hung those lips that I have kiss'd I know not how oft. Where be your gibes now, your gambols, your songs, your flashes of merriment that were wont to set the table on a roar? Not one now to mock your own grinning – quite chap-fall'n? Now get you to my lady's chamber, and tell her, let her paint an inch thick, to this favour she must come; make her laugh at that. Prithee, Horatio, tell me one thing.

Horatio

191 What's that, my lord?

Hamlet

Dost thou think Alexander look'd a this fashion i' th' earth?

Horatio

E'en so.

Hamlet

195 And smelt so? Pah!

[Throws down the skull.]

Horatio
 E'en so, my lord.
Hamlet
 To what base uses we may return, Horatio! Why
 may not imagination trace the noble dust of
 Alexander till 'a find it stopping a bung-hole?   199
Horatio
 'Twere to consider too curiously to consider so.
Hamlet
 No, faith, not a jot; but to follow him thither
 with modesty enough, and likelihood to lead it,
 as thus: Alexander died, Alexander was buried,
 Alexander returneth to dust; the dust is earth; of
 earth we make loam; and why of that loam
 whereto he was converted might they not stop a
 beer-barrel?   206
 Imperious Caesar, dead and turn'd to clay,
 Might stop a hole to keep the wind away.
 O, that that earth which kept the world in awe
 Should patch a wall t' expel the winter's flaw!   210
 But soft! but soft! awhile. Here comes the King.

[Enter the KING, QUEEN, LAERTES, *in funeral procession after
 the coffin, with* PRIEST *and* LORDS *attendant.]*

 The Queen, the courtiers. Who is this they
   follow?
 And with such maimed rites? This doth
   betoken
 The corse they follow did with desperate hand
 Fordo it own life. 'Twas of some estate.   215
 Couch we awhile and mark.

[Retiring with HORATIO.]*

Laertes
 What ceremony else?
Hamlet
 That is Laertes, a very noble youth. Mark,

Laertes
What ceremony else?

Priest
220   Her obsequies have been as far enlarg'd
As we have warrantise. Her death was doubtful;
And, but that great command o'ersways the
    order.
She should in ground unsanctified have lodg'd
Till the last trumpet; for charitable prayers,
Shards, flints, and pebbles, should be thrown
225   on her;
Yet here she is allow'd her virgin crants.
Her maiden strewments, and the bringing home
Of bell and burial.

Laertes
Must there no more be done?

Priest
                         No more be done.
230   We should profane the service of the dead
To sing sage requiem and such rest to her
As to peace-parted souls.

Laertes
                      Lay her i' th' earth;
And from her fair and unpolluted flesh
May violets spring! I tell thee, churlish priest,
235   A minist'ring angel shall my sister be
When thou liest howling.

Hamlet
                    What, the fair Ophelia!

Queen
Sweets to the sweet; farewell!

[Scattering flowers.]

I hop'd thou shouldst have been my Hamlet's
    wife;
I thought thy bride-bed to have deck'd, sweet
    maid,
And not have strew'd thy grave.

Laertes
                              O, treble woe 240
Fall ten times treble on that cursed head
Whose wicked deed thy most ingenious sense
Depriv'd thee of! Hold off the earth awhile,
Till I have caught her once more in mine arms.

                [Leaps into the grave.]

Now pile your dust upon the quick and dead,   245
Till of this flat a mountain you have made
T' o'er-top old Pelion or the skyish head
Of blue Olympus.
Hamlet [Advancing]
                              What is he whose grief
Bears such an emphasis, whose phrase of
   sorrow
Conjures the wand'ring stars, and makes them
   stand   250
Like wonder-wounded hearers? This is I,
Hamlet the Dane.   *[Leaps into the grave.]*
Laertes
The devil take thy soul!

                [Grappling with him.]

Hamlet
                        Thou pray'st not well.
I prithee take thy fingers from my throat;
For, though I am not splenitive and rash,   255
Yet have I in me something dangerous,
Which let thy wiseness fear. Hold off thy hand.
King
Pluck them asunder.
Queen
Hamlet! Hamlet!
All
Gentlemen!
Horatio
Good my lord, be quiet.

[The Attendants part them, and they come out of the grave.]

Hamlet

260   Why, I will fight with him upon this theme
          Until my eyelids will no longer wag.

Queen

          O my son, what theme?

Hamlet

          I lov'd Ophelia: forty thousand brothers
          Could not, with all their quantity of love,

265   Make up my sum. What wilt thou do for her?

King

          O, he is mad, Laertes.

Queen

          For love of God, forbear him.

Hamlet

          'Swounds, show me what th'owt do:
          Woo't weep, woo't fight, woo't fast, woo't tear
              thyself,

270   Woo't drink up eisel, eat a crocodile?
          I'll do't. Dost come here to whine?
          To outface me with leaping in her grave?
          Be buried quick with her, and so will I;
          And, if thou prate of mountains, let them
              throw

275   Millions of acres on us, till our ground,
          Singeing his pate against the burning zone,
          Make Ossa like a wart! Nay, an thou'lt mouth,
          I'll rant as well as thou.

Queen

                              This is mere madness;
          And thus awhile the fit will work on him;

280   Anon, as patient as the female dove
          When that her golden couplets are disclos'd,
          His silence will sit drooping.

Hamlet

                              Hear you, sir:
          What is the reason that you use me thus?

I lov'd you ever. But it is no matter.
Let Hercules himself do what he may,   285
The cat will mew, and dog will have his day.

[Exit.]

King

I pray thee, good Horatio, wait upon him.

[Exit HORATIO.*]*

[To LAERTES*]*
Strengthen your patience in our last night's
   speech;
We'll put the matter to the present push –
Good Gertrude, set some watch over your son. – 290
This grave shall have a living monument.
An hour of quiet shortly shall we see;
Till then in patience our proceeding be.

[Exeunt.]

Scene II

Elsinore. The Castle.

[Enter HAMLET *and* HORATIO.*]*

Hamlet
So much for this, sir, now shall you see the
     other.
You do remember all the circumstance?

Horatio
Remember it, my lord!

Hamlet
Sir, in my heart there was a kind of fighting
5   That would not let me sleep. Methought I lay
Worse than the mutines in the bilboes. Rashly.
And prais'd be rashness for it – let us know,
Our indiscretion sometime serves us well.
When our deep plots do pall, and that should
     learn us
10   There's a divinity that shapes our ends.
Rough-hew them how we will.

Horatio
                              That is most certain.

Hamlet
Up from my cabin,
My sea-gown scarf'd about me, in the dark
Grop'd I to find out them; had my desire;
15   Finger'd their packet, and in fine withdrew
To mine own room again, making so bold,
My fears forgetting manners, to unseal
Their grand commission; where I found,
     Horatio,
Ah, royal knavery! an exact command,
20   Larded with many several sorts of reasons,
Importing Denmark's health and England's
     too,
With, ho! such bugs and goblins in my life –
That, on the supervise, no leisure bated,

No, not to stay the grinding of the axe,
My head should be struck off.

Horatio

Is't possible?   25

Hamlet

Here's the commission; read it at more leisure.
But wilt thou hear now how I did proceed?

Horatio

I beseech you.

Hamlet

Being thus benetted round with villainies –
Ere I could make a prologue to my brains,   30
They had begun the play – I sat me down;
Devis'd a new commission; wrote it fair.
I once did hold it, as our statists do,
A baseness to write fair, and labour'd much
How to forget that learning; but, sir, now   35
It did me yeoman's service. Wilt thou know
Th' effect of what I wrote?

Horatio

Ay, good my lord.

Hamlet

An earnest conjuration from the King,
As England was his faithful tributary,
As love between them like the palm might
    flourish,   40
As peace should still her wheaten garland wear
And stand a comma 'tween their amities,
And many such like as-es of great charge,
That, on the view and knowing of these
    contents,
Without debatement further more or less,   45
He should those bearers put to sudden death,
Not shriving-time allow'd.

Horatio

How was this seal'd?

Hamlet

Why, even in that was heaven ordinant.

I had my father's signet in my purse,
50 Which was the model of that Danish seal;
Folded the writ up in the form of th' other;
Subscrib'd it, gave't th' impression, plac'd it
    safely,
The changeling never known. Now, the next
    day
Was our sea-fight; and what to this was sequent
55 Thou knowest already.

Horatio
So Guildenstern and Rosencrantz go to't.

Hamlet
Why, man, they did make love to this
    employment;
They are not near my conscience; their defeat
Does by their own insinuation grow:
60 'Tis dangerous when the baser nature comes
Between the pass and fell incensed points
Of mighty opposites.

Horatio
                    Why, what a king is this!

Hamlet
Does it not, think thee, stand me now upon –
He that hath kill'd my king and whor'd my
    mother;
65 Popp'd in between th' election and my hopes;
Thrown out his angle for my proper life,
And with such coz'nage – is't not perfect
    conscience
To quit him with this arm? And is't not to be
    damn'd
To let this canker of our nature come
70 In further evil?

Horatio
It must be shortly known to him from England
What is the issue of the business there.

Hamlet
It will be short; the interim is mine,

And a man's life's no more than to say 'one'.
But I am very sorry, good Horatio,   75
That to Laertes I forgot myself;
For by the image of my cause I see
The portraiture of his. I'll court his favours.
But sure the bravery of his grief did put me
Into a tow'ring passion.

Horatio

Peace; who comes here?   80

[Enter young OSRIC.]

Osric
Your lordship is right welcome back to
    Denmark.

Hamlet
I humbly thank you. sir *[Aside to HORATIO]* Dost
    know this water-fly?   83

Horatio
[Aside to HAMLET] No, my good lord.

Hamlet
[Aside to HORATIO] Thy state is the more gracious;
for 'tis a vice to know him. He hath much land,
and fertile. Let a beast be lord of beasts, and his
crib shall stand at the king's mess. 'Tis a chough;
but, as I say, spacious in the possession of dirt.

Osric
Sweet lord, if your lordship were at leisure, I
should impart a thing to you from his Majesty.   91

Hamlet
I will receive it, sir, with all diligence of spirit.
Put your bonnet to his right use; 'tis for the head.

Osric
I thank your lordship; it is very hot.

Hamlet
No, believe me, 'tis very cold; the wind is
northerly.   95

Osric
It is indifferent cold, my lord, indeed.

Hamlet

But yet methinks it is very sultry and hot for my
99   complexion.

Osric

Exceedingly, my lord; it is very sultry, as 'twere
– I cannot tell how. But, my lord, his Majesty
bade me signify to you that 'a has laid a great
wager on your head. Sir, this is the matter –

Hamlet

104   I beseech you, remember.

*[*HAMLET *moves him to put on his hat.]*

Osric

Nay, good my lord; for my ease, in good faith.
Sir, here is newly come to court Laertes; believe
me, an absolute gentleman, full of most excellent
differences, of very soft society and great showing.
Indeed, to speak feelingly of him, he is the card
or calendar of gentry, for you shall find in him
the continent of what part a gentleman would
111   see.

Hamlet

Sir, his definement suffers no perdition in you;
though, I know, to divide him inventorially would
dozy th' arithmetic of memory, and yet but yaw
neither in respect of his quick sail. But, in the
verity of extolment, I take him to be a soul of
great article, and his infusion of such dearth and
rareness as, to make true diction of him, his
semblable is his mirror, and who else would trace
him, his umbrage, nothing more.

Osric

120   Your lordship speaks most infallibly of him.

Hamlet

The concernancy, sir? Why do we wrap the
gentleman in our more rawer breath?

Osric

Sir?

Horatio

[*Aside to* HAMLET] Is't not possible to understand in another tongue? You will to't, sir, really.   125

Hamlet

What imports the nomination of this gentleman?

Osric

Of Laertes?

Horatio

[*Aside*] His purse is empty already; all's golden words are spent.   129

Hamlet

Of him, sir.

Osric

I know you are not ignorant –

Hamlet

I would you did, sir; yet, in faith, if you did, it would not much approve me. Well, sir.

Osric

You are not ignorant of what excellence Laertes is –   135

Hamlet

I dare not confess that, lest I should compare with him in excellence; but to know a man well were to know himself.   138

Osric

I mean, sir, for his weapon; but in the imputation laid on him by them, in his meed he's unfellowed.

Hamlet

What's his weapon?

Osric

Rapier and dagger.

Hamlet

That's two of his weapons – but well.   144

Osric

The King, sir, hath wager'd with him six Barbary horses; against the which he has impon'd, as I take it, six French rapiers and poniards, with

their assigns, as girdle, hangers, and so – three of
the carriages, in faith, are very dear to fancy, very
responsive to the hilts, most delicate carriages,
150   and of very liberal conceit.

Hamlet
What call you the carriages?

Horatio
[Aside to HAMLET*]* I knew you must be edified by
the margent ere you had done.

Osric
The carriages, sir, are the hangers.

Hamlet
The phrase would be more germane to the matter
if we could carry a cannon by our sides. I would
it might be hangers till then. But on: six Barbary
horses against six French swords, their assigns,
and three liberal conceited carriages; that's the
French bet against the Danish. Why is this all
160   impon'd, as you call it?

Osric
The King, sir, hath laid, sir, that in a dozen passes
between yourself and him he shall not exceed
you three hits; he hath laid on twelve for nine,
and it would come to immediate trial if your
165   lordship would vouchsafe the answer.

Hamlet
How if I answer no?

Osric
I mean, my lord, the opposition of your person
in trial.

Hamlet
Sir, I will walk here in the hall. If it please his
Majesty, it is the breathing time of day with me;
let the foils be brought, the gentleman willing,
and the King hold his purpose, I will win for him
an I can; if not, I will gain nothing but my shame
and the odd hits.

Osric

Shall I redeliver you e'en so?

Hamlet

To this effect, sir, after what flourish your nature
will.   176

Osric

I commend my duty to your lordship.

Hamlet

Yours, yours. *[Exit* OSRIC*]* He does well to commend
it himself; there are no tongues else for's turn.

Horatio

This lapwing runs away with the shell on his
head.   181

Hamlet

'A did comply, sir, with his dug before 'a suck'd
it. Thus has he, and many more of the same bevy,
that I know the drossy age dotes on, only got the
tune of the time and outward habit of encounter
– a kind of yesty collection, which carries them
through and through the most fann'd and
winnowed opinions; and do but blow them to
their trial, the bubblers are out.   188

[Enter a LORD.*]*

Lord

My lord, his Majesty commended him to you by
young Osric, who brings back to him that you
attend him in the hall. He sends to know if your
pleasure hold to play with Laertes, or that you
will take longer time.

Hamlet

I am constant to my purposes; they follow the
king's pleasure: if his fitness speaks, mine is ready
now – or whensoever, provided I be so able as now. 195

Lord

The King and Queen and all are coming down.

Hamlet

In happy time.

Lord
The Queen desires you to use some gentle enter-
199   tainment to Laertes before you fall to play.
Hamlet
She well instructs me. *[Exit* LORD.*]*
Horatio
You will lose this wager, my lord.
Hamlet
I do not think so; since he went into
France I have been in continual practice. I shall
win at the odds. But thou wouldst not think how
205   ill all's here about my heart; but it is no matter.
Horatio
Nay, good my lord –
Hamlet
It is but foolery; but it is such a kind of gain-giving
as would perhaps trouble a woman.
Horatio
If your mind dislike anything, obey it. I will fore-
210   stall their repair hither, and say you are not fit.
Hamlet
Not a whit, we defy augury: there is a special
providence in the fall of a sparrow. If it be now,
'tis not to come; if it be not to come, it will be
now; if it be not now, yet it will come – the readi-
ness is all. Since no man owes of aught he leaves,
what is't to leave betimes? Let be.

*[A table prepared. Trumpets, Drums, and Officers with cush-
ions, foils and daggers. Enter* KING, QUEEN, LAERTES, *and all
the State.]*

King
Come, Hamlet, come, and take this hand from
me. *[The* KING *puts* LAERTES's *hand into* HAMLET's.*]*
Hamlet
Give me your pardon, sir. I have done you wrong;
But pardon 't, as you are a gentleman.
220   This presence knows,

And you must needs have heard how I am
  punish'd
With a sore distraction. What I have done
That might your nature, honour, and
  exception,
Roughly awake, I here proclaim was madness.
Was't Hamlet wrong'd Laertes? Never Hamlet.   225
If Hamlet from himself be ta'en away,
And when he's not himself does wrong Laertes,
Then Hamlet does it not, Hamlet denies it.
Who does it, then? His madness. If't be so,
Hamlet is of the faction that is wrong'd;   230
His madness is poor Hamlet's enemy.
Sir, in this audience,
Let my disclaiming from a purpos'd evil
Free me so far in your most generous thoughts
That I have shot my arrow o'er the house   235
And hurt my brother.

Laertes
            I am satisfied in nature,
Whose motive in this case should stir me most
To my revenge; but in my terms of honour
I stand aloof, and will no reconcilement
Till by some elder masters of known honour   240
I have a voice and precedent of peace
To keep my name ungor'd – but till that time
I do receive your offer'd love like love,
And will not wrong it.

Hamlet
            I embrace it freely;
And will this brother's wager frankly play.   245
Give us the foils. Come on.

Laertes
              Come, one for me.

Hamlet
I'll be your foil, Laertes; in mine ignorance
Your skill shall, like a star i' th' darkest night,
Stick fiery off indeed.

Laertes

You mock me, sir.

Hamlet

250   No, by this hand.

King

Give them the foils, young Osric. Cousin
    Hamlet,
You know the wager?

Hamlet

Very well, my lord;
Your Grace has laid the odds a' th' weaker side.

King

I do not fear it: I have seen you both;
255   But since he's better'd, we have therefore odds.

Laertes

This is too heavy; let me see another.

Hamlet

This likes me well. These foils have all a length?
[They prepare to play.]

Osric

Ay, my good lord.

King

Set me the stoups of wine upon that table.
260   If Hamlet give the first or second hit,
Or quit in answer of the third exchange,
Let all the battlements their ordnance fire;
The King shall drink to Hamlet's better breath,
And in the cup an union shall he throw,
265   Richer than that which four successive kings
In Denmark's crown have worn. Give me the
    cups;
And let the kettle to the trumpet speak,
The trumpet to the cannoneer without,
The cannons to the heavens, the heaven to earth,
270   'Now the King drinks to Hamlet'. Come, begin –
And you, the judges, bear a wary eye.

Hamlet

Come on, sir.

Laertes
  Come, my lord.   *[They play.]*
Hamlet
  One.
Laertes
  No.
Hamlet
  Judgment?
Osric
  A hit, a very palpable hit.
Laertes
  Well, again.
King
  Stay, give me drink. Hamlet, this pearl is thine;
  Here's to thy health.

  [Drum, trumpets, and shot.]

  Give him the cup.   275
Hamlet
  I'll play this bout first; set it by awhile.
  Come.   *[They play.]*
  Another hit; what say you?
Laertes
  A touch, a touch, I do confess't.
King
  Our son shall win.
Queen
  He's fat, and scant of breath.
  Here, Hamlet, take my napkin, rub thy brows.   280
  The Queen carouses to thy fortune, Hamlet.
Hamlet
  Good madam!
King
  Gertrude, do not drink.
Queen
  I will, my lord; I pray you pardon me.
King [Aside]
  It is the poison'd cup; it is too late.

Hamlet
285   I dare not drink yet, madam; by and by.
Queen
    Come, let me wipe thy face.
Laertes
    My lord, I'll hit him now.
King
                      I do not think't.
Laertes [Aside]
    And yet it is almost against my conscience.
Hamlet
    Come, for the third. Laertes, you do but dally;
290   I pray you pass with your best violence;
    I am afeard you make a wanton of me.
Laertes
    Say you so? Come on. *[They play.]*
Osric
    Nothing, neither way.
Laertes
    Have at you now! *[*LAERTES *wounds* HAMLET*: then, in scuffling, they change rapiers, and* HAMLET *wounds* LAERTES.*]*
King
    Part them; they are incens'd.
Hamlet
    Nay, come again. *[The* QUEEN *falls.]*
Osric
295   Look to the Queen there, ho!
Horatio
    They bleed on both sides. How is it, my lord?
Osric
    How is't, Laertes?
Laertes
    Why, as a woodcock, to mine own springe, Osric;
    I am justly kill'd with mine own treachery.
Hamlet
    How does the Queen?

King

    She swoons to see them bleed.   300

Queen

    No, no, the drink, the drink! O my dear
      Hamlet!
    The drink, the drink! I am poison'd. *[Dies.]*

Hamlet

    O, villainy! Ho! let the door be lock'd
    Treachery! seek it out. *[*LAERTES *falls.]*

Laertes

    It is here, Hamlet. Hamlet, thou art slain;   305
    No med'cine in the world can do thee good;
    In thee there is not half an hour's life;
    The treacherous instrument is in thy hand,
    Unbated and envenom'd. The foul practice
    Hath turn'd itself on me; lo, here I lie,   310
    Never to rise again. They mother's poison'd.
    I can no more. The King, the King's to blame.

Hamlet

    The point envenom'd too!
    Then, venom, to thy work. *[Stabs the* KING.*]*

All

    Treason! treason!   315

King

    O, yet defend me, friends: I am but hurt.

Hamlet

    Here, thou incestous, murd'rous, damned Dane,
    Drink off this potion. Is thy union here?
    Follow my mother. *[*KING *dies.]*

Laertes

                He is justly serv'd:
    It is a poison temper'd by himself.   320
    Exchange forgiveness with me, noble Hamlet.
    Mine and my father's death come not upon
      thee,
    Nor thine on me! *[Dies.]*

Hamlet

    Heaven make thee free of it! I follow thee.

325 I am dead, Horatio. Wretched queen, adieu!
You that look pale and tremble at this chance,
That are but mutes or audience to this act,
Had I but time, as this fell sergeant Death
Is strict in his arrest, O, I could tell you –
330 But let it be. Horatio. I am dead:
Thou livest; report me and my cause aright
To the unsatisfied.

Horatio
Never believe it.
I am more an antique Roman than a Dane;
Here's yet some liquor left.

Hamlet
As th'art a man,
335 Give me the cup. Let go. By heaven, I'll ha't.
O God! Horatio, what a wounded name,
Things standing thus unknown, shall live
behind me!
If thou didst ever hold me in thy heart,
Absent thee from felicity awhile,
340 And in this harsh world draw thy breath in pain,
To tell my story.

[March afar off, and shot within.]

What warlike noise is this?

Osric
Young Fortinbras, with conquest come from
Poland,
To th' ambassadors of England gives
This warlike volley.

Hamlet
O, I die, Horatio!
345 The potent poison quite o'er-crows my spirit.
I cannot live to hear the news from England,
But I do prophesy th' election lights
On Fortinbras; he has my dying voice.
So tell him, with th' occurrents, more and less,
350 Which have solicited – the rest is silence.

[Dies.]

Horatio
> Now cracks a noble heart. Good night, sweet
> > prince.
> And flights of angels sing thee to thy rest!

[March within.]

> Why does the drum come hither?

[Enter FORTINBRAS *and* ENGLISH AMBASSADORS, *with drum,*
colours, and ATTENDANTS.*]*

Fortinbras
> Where is this sight?
Horatio
> > > What is it you would see?
> If aught of woe or wonder, cease your search.   355
Fortinbras
> This quarry cries on havoc. O proud death,
> What feast is toward in thine eternal cell
> That thou so many princes at a shot
> So bloodily hast struck?
Ambassador
> > > > The sight is dismal;
> And our affairs from England come too late: 360
> The ears are senseless that should give us
> > hearing
> To tell him his commandment is fulfill'd,
> That Rosencrantz and Guildenstern are dead.
> Where should we have our thanks?
Horatio
> > > > Not from his mouth,
> Had it th' ability of life to thank you: 365
> He never gave commandment for their death.
> But since, so jump upon this bloody question,
> You from the Polack wars, and you from
> > England,
> Are here arrived, give order that these bodies
> High on a stage be placed to the view;   370

And let me speak to th' yet unknowing world
How these things came about. So shall you hear
Of carnal, bloody, and unnatural acts;
Of accidental judgments, casual slaughters;
375   Of deaths put on by cunning and forc'd cause;
And, in this upshot, purposes mistook
Fall'n on th' inventors' heads – all this can I
Truly deliver.

Fortinbras

                Let us haste to hear it,
And call the noblest to the audience.
380   For me, with sorrow I embrace my fortune;
I have some rights of memory in this kingdom,
Which now to claim my vantage doth invite
      me.

Horatio

Of that I shall have also cause to speak,
And from his mouth whose voice will draw on
      more.
385   But let this same be presently perform'd,
Even while men's minds are wild, lest more
      mischance
On plots and errors happen.

Fortinbras

                    Let four captains
Bear Hamlet like a soldier to the stage;
For he was likely, had he been put on,
390   To have prov'd most royal; and for his passage
The soldier's music and the rite of war
Speak loudly for him.
Take up the bodies. Such a sight as this
Becomes the field, but here shows much amiss.
395   Go, bid the soldiers shoot.

[Exeunt marching. A peal of ordnance shot off.]

Shakespeare: Words and Phrases

adapted from the Collins English Dictionary

abate 1 VERB to abate here means to lessen or diminish ❑ *There lives within the very flame of love/A kind of wick or snuff that will abate it* (*Hamlet 4.7*) 2 VERB to abate here means to shorten ❑ *Abate thy hours* (*A Midsummer Night's Dream 3.2*) 3 VERB to abate here means to deprive ❑ *She hath abated me of half my train* (*King Lear 2.4*)

abjure VERB to abjure means to renounce or give up ❑ *this rough magic I here abjure* (*Tempest 5.1*)

abroad ADV abroad means elsewhere or everywhere ❑ *You have heard of the news abroad* (*King Lear 2.1*)

abrogate VERB to abrogate means to put an end to ❑ *so it shall praise you to abrogate scurrility* (*Love's Labours Lost 4.2*)

abuse 1 NOUN abuse in this context means deception or fraud ❑ *What should this mean? Are all the rest come back?/Or is it some abuse, and no such thing?* (*Hamlet 4.7*) 2 NOUN an abuse in this context means insult or offence ❑ *I will be deaf to pleading and excuses/Nor tears nor prayers shall purchase our abuses* (*Romeo and Juliet 3.1*) 3 NOUN an abuse in this context means using something improperly ❑ *we'll digest/Th'abuse*

of distance (*Henry II Chorus*) 4 NOUN an abuse in this context means doing something which is corrupt or dishonest ❑ *Come, bring them away: if these be good people in a commonweal that do nothing but their abuses in common houses, I know no law: bring them away.* (*Measure for Measure 2.1*)

abuser NOUN the abuser here is someone who betrays, a betrayer ❑ *I ... do attach thee/For an abuser of the world* (*Othello 1.2*)

accent NOUN accent here means language ❑ *In states unborn, and accents yet unknown* (*Julius Caesar 3.1*)

accident NOUN an accident in this context is an event or something that happened ❑ *think no more of this night's accidents* (*A Midsummer Night's Dream 4.1*)

accommodate VERB to accommodate in this context means to equip or to give someone the equipment to do something ❑ *The safer sense will ne'er accommodate/His master thus.* (*King Lear 4.6*)

according ADJ according means sympathetic or ready to agree ❑ *within the scope of choice/Lies* *my consent and fair according voice* (*Romeo and Juliet* 1.2)

account NOUN account often means judgement (by God) or reckoning ❑ *No reckoning made, but sent to my account/ With all my imperfections on my head* (*Hamlet* 1.5)

accountant ADJ accountant here means answerable or accountable ❑ *his offence is… /Accountant to the law* (*Measure for Measure* 2.4)

ace NOUN ace here means one or first referring to the lowest score on a dice ❑ *No die, but an ace, for him; for he is but one./ Less than an ace, man; for he is dead; he is nothing.* (*A Midsummer Night's Dream* 5.1)

acquit VERB here acquit means to be rid of or free of. It is related to the verb quit ❑ *I am glad I am so acquit of this tinderbox* (*The Merry Wives of Windsor* 1.3)

afeard ADJ afeard means afraid or frightened ❑ *Nothing afeard of what thyself didst make* (*Macbeth* 1.3)

affiance NOUN affiance means confidence or trust ❑ *O how hast thou with jealousy infected/ The sweetness of affiance* (*Henry V* 2.2)

affinity NOUN in this context, affinity means important connections, or relationships with important people ❑ *The Moor replies/ That he you hurt is of great fame in Cyprus,/ And great affinity* (*Othello* 3.1)

agnize VERB to agnize is an old word that means that you recognize or acknowledge something ❑ *I do agnize/A natural and prompt alacrity I find in hardness* (*Othello* 1.3)

ague NOUN an ague is a fever in which the patient has hot and cold

shivers one after the other ❑ *This is some monster of the isle with four legs, who hath got … an ague* (*The Tempest* 2.2)

alarm, alarum NOUN an alarm or alarum is a call to arms or a signal for soldiers to prepare to fight ❑ *Whence cometh this alarum and the noise?* (*Henry VI part I* 1.4)

Albion NOUN Albion is another word for England ❑ *but I will sell my dukedom,/ To buy a slobbery and a dirty farm In that nook-shotten isle of Albion* (*Henry V* 3.5)

all of all PHRASE all of all means everything, or the sum of all things ❑ *The very all of all* (*Love's Labours Lost* 5.1)

amend VERB amend in this context means to get better or to heal ❑ *at his touch… They presently amend* (*Macbeth* 4.3)

anchor VERB if you anchor on something you concentrate on it or fix on it ❑ *My invention … Anchors on Isabel* (*Measure for Measure* 2.4)

anon ADV anon was a common word for soon ❑ *You shall see anon how the murderer gets the love of Gonzago's wife* (*Hamlet* 3.2)

antic 1 ADJ antic here means weird or strange ❑ *I'll charm the air to give a sound/ While you perform your antic round* (*Macbeth* 4.1) 2 NOUN in this context antic means a clown or a strange, unattractive creature ❑ *If black, why nature, drawing an antic,/ Made a foul blot* (*Much Ado About Nothing* 3.1)

apace ADV apace was a common word for quickly ❑ *Come apace* (*As You Like It* 3.3)

apparel NOUN apparel means clothes or clothing ❑ *one suit of apparel* (*Hamlet 3.2*)

appliance NOUN appliance here means cure ❑ *Diseases desperate grown/ By desperate appliance are relieved* (*Hamlet 4.3*)

argument NOUN argument here means a topic of conversation or the subject ❑ *Why 'tis the rarest argument of wonder that hath shot out in our latter times* (*All's Well That Ends Well 2.3*)

arrant ADJ arrant means absolute, complete. It strengthens the meaning of a noun ❑ *Fortune, that arrant whore* (*King Lear 2.4*)

arras NOUN an arras is a tapestry, a large cloth with a picture sewn on it using coloured thread ❑ *Behind the arras I'll convey myself/ To hear the process* (*Hamlet 3.3*)

art 1 NOUN art in this context means knowledge ❑ *Their malady convinces/ The great essay of art* (*Macbeth 4.3*) 2 NOUN art can also mean skill as it does here ❑ *He … gave you such a masterly report/ For art and exercise in your defence* (*Hamlet 4.7*) 3 NOUN art here means magic ❑ *Now I want/ Spirits to enforce, art to enchant* (*The Tempest 5 Epilogue*)

assay 1 NOUN an assay was an attempt, a try ❑ *Make assay./ Bow, stubborn knees* (*Hamlet 3.3*) 2 NOUN assay can also mean a test or a trial ❑ *he hath made assay of her virtue* (*Measure for Measure 3.1*)

attend (on/upon) VERB attend on means to wait for or to expect ❑ *Tarry I here, I but attend on death* (*Two Gentlemen of Verona 3.1*)

auditor NOUN an auditor was a member of an audience or someone who listens ❑ *I'll be an auditor* (*A Midsummer Night's Dream 3.1*)

aught NOUN aught was a common word which meant anything ❑ *if my love thou holdest at aught* (*Hamlet 4.3*)

aunt 1 NOUN an aunt was another word for an old woman and also means someone who talks a lot or a gossip ❑ *The wisest aunt telling the saddest tale* (*A Midsummer Night's Dream 2.1*) 2 NOUN aunt could also mean a mistress or a prostitute ❑ *the thrush and the jay/ Are summer songs for me and my aunts/ While we lie tumbling in the hay* (*The Winter's Tale 4.3*)

avaunt EXCLAM avaunt was a common word which meant go away ❑ *Avaunt, you curs!* (*King Lear 3.6*)

aye ADV here aye means always or ever ❑ *Whose state and honour I for aye allow* (*Richard II 5.2*)

baffle VERB baffle meant to be disgraced in public or humiliated ❑ *I am disgraced, impeached, and baffled here* (*Richard II 1.1*)

bald ADJ bald means trivial or silly ❑ *I knew 'twould be a bald conclusion* (*The Comedy of Errors 2.2*)

ban NOUN a ban was a curse or an evil spell ❑ *Sometimes with lunatic bans... Enforce their charity* (*King Lear 2.3*)

barren ADJ barren meant empty or hollow ❑ *now I let go your hand, I am barren.* (*Twelfth Night 1.3*)

base ADJ base is an adjective that means unworthy or dishonourable ❑ *civet is of a baser birth than tar* (*As You Like It 3.2*)

base 1 ADJ base can also mean of low social standing or someone who was not part of the ruling class ❑ *Why brand they us with 'base'?* (*King Lear 1.2*) 2 ADJ here base means poor quality ❑ *Base cousin,/ Darest thou break first?* (*Two Noble Kinsmen 3.3*)

bawdy NOUN bawdy means obscene or rude ❑ *Bloody, bawdy villain!* (*Hamlet 2.2*)

bear in hand PHRASE bear in hand means taken advantage of or fooled ❑ *This I made good to you In our last conference, passed in probation with you/ How you were borne in hand* (*Macbeth 3.1*)

beard VERB to beard someone was to oppose or confront them ❑ *Com'st thou to beard me in Denmark?* (*Hamlet 2.2*)

beard, in one's PHRASE if you say something in someone's beard you say it to their face ❑ *I will verify as much in his beard* (*Henry V 3.2*)

beaver NOUN a beaver was a visor on a battle helmet ❑ *O yes, my lord, he wore his beaver up* (*Hamlet 1.2*)

become VERB if something becomes you it suits you or is appropriate to you ❑ *Nothing in his life became him like the leaving it* (*Macbeth 1.4*)

bed, brought to PHRASE to be brought to bed means to give birth ❑ *His wife but yesternight was brought to bed* (*Titus Andronicus 4.2*)

bedabbled ADJ if something is bedabbled it is sprinkled ❑ *Bedabbled with the dew, and torn with briers* (*A Midsummer Night's Dream 3.2*)

Bedlam NOUN Bedlam was a word used for Bethlehem Hospital which was a place the insane were sent to ❑ *The country give me proof and precedent/ Of Bedlam beggars* (*King Lear 2.3*)

bed-swerver NOUN a bed-swerver was someone who was unfaithful in marriage, an adulterer ❑ *she's/ A bed-swerver* (*Winter's Tale 2.1*)

befall 1 VERB to befall is to happen, occur or take place ❑ *In this same interlude it doth befall/ That I present a wall* (*A Midsummer Night's Dream 5.1*) 2 VERB to befall can also mean to happen to someone or something ❑ *fair befall thee and thy noble house* (*Richard III 1.3*)

behoof NOUN behoof was an advantage or benefit ❑ *All our surgeons/ Convent in their behoof* (*Two Noble Kinsmen 1.4*)

beldam NOUN a beldam was a witch or old woman ❑ *Have I not reason, beldams as you are?* (*Macbeth 3.5*)

belike ADV belike meant probably, perhaps or presumably ❑ *belike he likes it not* (*Hamlet 3.2*)

bent 1 NOUN bent means a preference or a direction ❑ *Let me work,/ For I can give his humour true bent,/ And I will bring him to the Capitol* (*Julius Caesar 2.1*) 2 ADJ if you are bent on something you are determined to do it ❑ *for now I am bent to know/ By the worst means the worst.* (*Macbeth 3.4*)

beshrew VERB beshrew meant to curse or wish evil on someone ❑ *much beshrew my manners and my pride/ If Hermia meant to say Lysander lied* (*A Midsummer Night's Dream 2.2*)

betime (s) ADV betime means early ❏ *To business that we love we rise betime* (*Antony and Cleopatra* 4.4)

bevy NOUN bevy meant type or sort, it was also used to mean company ❏ *many more of the same bevy* (*Hamlet* 5.2)

blazon VERB to blazon something meant to display or show it ❏ *that thy skill be more to blazon it* (*Romeo and Juliet* 2.6)

blind ADJ if you are blind when you do something you are reckless or do not care about the consequences ❏ *are you yet to your own souls so blind/That two you will war with God by murdering me* (*Richard III* 1.4)

bombast NOUN bombast was wool stuffing (used in a cushion for example) and so it came to mean padded out or long-winded. Here it means someone who talks a lot about nothing in particular ❏ *How now my sweet creature of bombast* (*Henry IV part I* 2.4)

bond 1 NOUN a bond is a contract or legal deed ❏ *Well, then, your bond, and let me see* (*Merchant of Venice* 1.3) 2 NOUN bond could also mean duty or commitment ❏ *I love your majesty/According to my bond* (*King Lear* 1.1)

bottom NOUN here bottom means essence, main point or intent ❏ *Now I see/The bottom of your purpose* (*All's Well That Ends Well* 3.7)

bounteously ADV bounteously means plentifully, abundantly ❏ *I prithee, and I'll pay thee bounteously* (*Twelfth Night* 1.2)

brace 1 NOUN a brace is a couple or two ❏ *Have lost a brace of kinsmen* (*Romeo and Juliet* 5.3) 2 NOUN if you are in a brace position it means you are ready ❏ *For that it stands not in such warlike brace* (*Othello* 1.3)

brand VERB to mark permanently like the markings on cattle ❏ *the wheeled seat/Of fortunate Caesar ... branded his baseness that ensued* (*Anthony and Cleopatra* 4.14)

brave ADJ brave meant fine, excellent or splendid ❏ *O brave new world/That has such people in't* (*The Tempest* 5.1)

brine NOUN brine is sea-water ❏ *He shall drink nought brine, for I'll not show him/Where the quick freshes are* (*The Tempest* 3.2)

brow NOUN brow in this context means appearance ❏ *doth hourly grow/Out of his brows* (*Hamlet* 3.3)

burden 1 NOUN the burden here is a chorus ❏ *I would sing my song without a burden* (*As You Like It* 3.2) 2 NOUN burden means load or weight (this is the current meaning) ❏ *the scarfs and the bannerets about thee did manifoldly dissuade me from believing thee a vessel of too great a burden* (*All's Well that Ends Well* 2.3)

buttons, in one's PHRASE this is a phrase that means clear, easy to see ❏ *Tis in his buttons he will carry't* (*The Merry Wives of Windsor* 3.2)

cable NOUN cable here means scope or reach ❏ *The law ... Will give her cable* (*Othello* 1.2)

cadent ADJ if something is cadent it is falling or dropping ❏ *With cadent tears fret channels in her cheeks* (*King Lear* 1.4)

canker VERB to canker is to decay, become corrupt ❑ *And, as with age his body uglier grows,/So his mind cankers* (*The Tempest 4.1*)

canon, from the PHRASE from the canon is an expression meaning out of order, improper ❑ *Twas from the canon* (*Coriolanus 3.1*)

cap-a-pie ADV cap-a-pie means from head to foot, completely ❑ *I am courtier cap-a-pie* (*The Winter's Tale 4.4*)

carbonadoed ADJ if something is carbonadoed it is cut or scored (scratched) with a knife ❑ *it is your carbonadoed* (*All's Well That Ends Well 4.5*)

carouse VERB to carouse is to drink at length, party ❑ *They cast their caps up and carouse together* (*Anthony and Cleopatra 4.12*)

carrack NOUN a carrack was a large old ship, a galleon ❑ *Faith, he tonight hath boarded a land-carrack* (*Othello 1.2*)

cassock NOUN a cassock here means a military cloak, long coat ❑ *half of the which dare not shake the snow from off their cassocks lest they shake themselves to pieces* (*All's Well That Ends Well 4.3*)

catastrophe NOUN catastrophe here means conclusion or end ❑ *pat he comes, like the catastrophe of the old comedy* (*King Lear 1.2*)

cautel NOUN a cautel was a trick or a deceptive act ❑ *Perhaps he loves you now/And now no soil not cautel doth besmirch* (*Hamlet 1.2*)

celerity NOUN celerity was a common word for speed, swiftness ❑ *Hence hath offence his quick celerity/When it is borne in high authority* (*Measure for Measure 4.2*)

chafe NOUN chafe meant anger or temper ❑ *this Herculean Roman does become/The carriage of his chafe* (*Anthony and Cleopatra 1.3*)

chanson NOUN chanson was an old word for a song ❑ *The first row of the pious chanson will show you more* (*Hamlet 2.2*)

chapman NOUN a chapman was a trader or merchant ❑ *Not uttered by base sale of chapman's tongues* (*Love's Labours Lost 2.1*)

chaps, chops NOUN chaps (and chops) was a word for jaws ❑ *Which ne'er shook hands nor bade farewell to him/Till he unseamed him from the nave to th' chops* (*Macbeth 1.2*)

chattels NOUN chattels were your moveable possessions. The word is used in the traditional marriage ceremony ❑ *She is my goods, my chattels* (*The Taming of the Shrew 3.3*)

chide VERB if you are chided by someone you are told off or reprimanded ❑ *Now I but chide, but I should use thee worse* (*A Midsummer Night's Dream 3.2*)

chinks NOUN chinks was a word for cash or money ❑ *he that can lay hold of her/Shall have the chinks* (*Romeo and Juliet 1.5*)

choleric ADJ if something was called choleric it meant that they were quick to get angry ❑ *therewithal unruly waywardness that infirm and choleric years bring with them* (*King Lear 1.1*)

chuff NOUN a chuff was a miser,

someone who clings to his or her money ❏ *ye fat chuffs* (*Henry IV part I 2.2*)

cipher NOUN cipher here means nothing ❏ *Mine were the very cipher of a function* (*Measure for Measure 2.2*)

circummured ADJ circummured means that something is surrounded with a wall ❏ *He hath a garden circummured with brick* (*Measure for Measure 4.1*)

civet NOUN a civet is a type of scent or perfume ❏ *Give me an ounce of civet* (*King Lear 4.6*)

clamorous ADJ clamorous means noisy or boisterous ❏ *Be clamorous and leap all civil bounds* (*Twelfth Night 1.4*)

clangour, clangor NOUN clangour is a word that means ringing (the sound that bells make) ❏ *Like to a dismal clangour heard from far* (*Henry VI part III 2.3*)

cleave VERB if you cleave to something you stick to it or are faithful to it ❏ *Thy thoughts I cleave to* (*The Tempest 4.1*)

clock and clock, 'twixt PHRASE from hour to hour, without stopping or continuously ❏ *To weep 'twixt clock and clock* (*Cymbeline 3.4*)

close ADJ here close means hidden ❏ *Stand close; this is the same Athenian* (*A Midsummer Night's Dream 3.2*)

cloud NOUN a cloud on your face means that you have a troubled, unhappy expression ❏ *He has cloud in's face* (*Anthony and Cleopatra 3.2*)

cloy VERB if you cloy an appetite you satisfy it ❏ *Other women cloy/The appetites they feed* (*Anthony and Cleopatra 2.2*)

cock-a-hoop, set PHRASE if you set cock-a-hoop you become free of everything ❏ *You will set cock-a-hoop* (*Romeo and Juliet 1.5*)

colours NOUN colours is a word used to describe battle-flags or banners. Sometimes we still say that we nail our colours to the mast if we are stating which team or side of an argument we support ❏ *the approbation of those that weep this lamentable divorce under her colours* (*Cymbeline 1.5*)

combustion NOUN combustion was a word meaning disorder or chaos ❏ *prophesying ... Of dire combustion and confused events* (*Macbeth 2.3*)

comely ADJ if you are or something is comely you or it is lovely, beautiful, graceful ❏ *O, what a world is this, when what is comely/Envenoms him that bears it!* (*As You Like It 2.3*)

commend VERB if you commend yourself to someone you send greetings to them ❏ *Commend me to my brother* (*Measure for Measure 1.4*)

compact NOUN a compact is an agreement or a contract ❏ *what compact mean you to have with us?* (*Julius Caesar 3.1*)

compass 1 NOUN here compass means range or scope ❏ *you would sound me from my lowest note to the top of my compass* (*Hamlet 3.2*) 2 VERB to compass here means to achieve, bring about or make happen ❏ *How now shall this be compassed?/Canst thou bring me to the party?* (*Tempest 3.2*)

comptible ADJ comptible is an old word meaning sensitive ❏ *I am very comptible, even to the least sinister usage.* (*Twelfth Night 1.5*)

confederacy NOUN a confederacy is a group of people usually joined together to commit a crime. It is another word for a conspiracy ❏ *Lo, she is one of this confederacy!* (*A Midsummer Night's Dream 3.2*)

confound VERB if you confound something you confuse it or mix it up; it also means to stop or prevent ❏ *A million fail, confounding oath on oath.* (*A Midsummer Night's Dream 3.2*)

contagion NOUN contagion is an old word for disease or poison ❏ *hell itself breathes out/Contagion to this world* (*Hamlet 3.2*)

contumely NOUN contumely is an old word for an insult ❏ *the proud man's contumely* (*Hamlet 3.1*)

counterfeit 1 VERB if you counterfeit something you copy or imitate it ❏ *Meantime your cheeks do counterfeit our roses* (*Henry VI part I 2.4*) 2 VERB in this context counterfeit means to pretend or make believe ❏ *I will counterfeit the bewitchment of some popular man* (*Coriolanus*)

coz NOUN coz was a shortened form of the word cousin ❏ *sweet my coz, be merry* (*As You Like It 1.2*)

cozenage NOUN cozenage is an old word meaning cheating or a deception ❏ *Thrown out his angle for my proper life,/ And with such coz'nage* (*Hamlet 5.2*)

crave VERB crave used to mean to beg or request ❏ *I crave your pardon* (*The Comedy of Errors 1.2*)

crotchet NOUN crotchets are strange ideas or whims ❏ *thou hast some strange crotchets in thy head now* (*The Merry Wives of Windsor 2.1*)

cuckold NOUN a cuckold is a man whose wife has been unfaithful to him ❏ *As there is no true cuckold but calamity* (*Twelfth Night 1.5*)

cuffs, go to PHRASE this phrase meant to fight ❏ *the player went to cuffs in the question* (*Hamlet 2.2*)

cup VERB in this context cup is a verb which means to pour drink or fill glasses with alcohol ❏ *cup us til the world go round* (*Anthony and Cleopatra 2.7*)

cur NOUN cur is an insult meaning dog and is also used to mean coward ❏ *Out, dog! out, cur! Thou drivest me past the bounds/ Of maiden's patience* (*A Midsummer Night's Dream 3.2*)

curiously ADV in this context curiously means carefully or skilfully ❏ *The sleeves curiously cut* (*The Taming of the Shrew 4.3*)

curry VERB curry means to flatter or to praise someone more than they are worth ❏ *I would curry with Master Shallow that no man could better command his servants* (*Henry IV part II 5.1*)

custom NOUN custom is a habit or a usual practice ❏ *Hath not old custom made this life more sweet/ Than that of painted pomp?* (*As You Like It 2.1*)

cutpurse NOUN a cutpurse is an old word for a thief. Men used to carry their money in small bags (purse) that hung from their belts; thieves would cut the purse from the belt and steal their money ❏ *A cutpurse of the empire and the rule* (*Hamlet 3.4*)

dainty ADJ dainty used to mean splendid, fine ❏ *Why, that's my dainty Ariel!* (*Tempest 5.1*)

dally VERB if you dally with something you play with it or tease it ❏ *They that dally nicely with words may quickly make them wanton* (*Twelfth Night 3.1*)

damask COLOUR damask is a light-red or pink colour ❏ *Twas just the difference/Betwixt the constant red and mingled damask* (*As You Like It 3.5*)

dare 1 VERB dare means to challenge or, confront ❏ *He goes before me, and still dares me on* (*A Midsummer Night's Dream 3.3*) 2 VERB dare in this context means to present, deliver or inflict ❏ *all that fortune, death, and danger dare* (*Hamlet 4.4*)

darkly ADV darkly was used in this context to mean secretly or cunningly ❏ *I will go darkly to work with her* (*Measure for Measure 5.1*)

daw NOUN a daw was a slang term for idiot or fool (after the bird jackdaw which was famous for its stupidity) ❏ *Yea, just so much as you may take upon a knife's point and choke a daw withal* (*Much Ado About Nothing 3.1*)

debile ADJ debile meant weak or feeble ❏ *And debile minister great power* (*All's Well That Ends Well 2.3*)

deboshed ADJ deboshed was another way of saying corrupted or debauched ❏ *Men so disordered, deboshed and bold* (*King Lear 1.4*)

decoct VERB to decoct was to heat up, warm something ❏ *Can sodden water,/A drench for sur-reined jades*

... Decoct their cold blood to such valiant heat? (*Henry V 3.5*)

deep-revolving ADJ deep-revolving here uses the idea that you turn something over in your mind when you are thinking hard about it and so means deep-thinking, meditating ❏ *The deep-revolving Buckingham/No more shall be the neighbour to my counsels* (*Richard III 4.2*)

defect NOUN defect here means shortcoming or something that is not right ❏ *Being unprepared/Our will became the servant to defect* (*Macbeth 2.1*)

degree 1 NOUN degree here means rank, standing or station ❏ *Should a like language use to all degrees,/ And mannerly distinguishment leave out/Betwixt the prince and beggar* (*The Winter's Tale 2.1*) 2 NOUN in this context, degree means extent or measure ❏ *her offence/Must be of such unnatural degree* (*King Lear 1.1*)

deify VERB if you deify something or someone you worship it or them as a God ❏ *all.. deifying the name of Rosalind* (*As You Like It 3.2*)

delated ADJ delated here means detailed ❏ *the scope/Of these delated articles* (*Hamlet 1.2*)

delicate ADJ if something was described as delicate it meant it was of fine quality or valuable ❏ *thou wast a spirit too delicate* (*The Tempest 1.2*)

demise VERB in this context demise means to transmit, give or convey ❏ *what state ... Canst thou demise to any child of mine?* (*Richard III 4.4*)

deplore VERB to deplore means to express with grief or sorrow ❑ *Never more/ Will I my master's tears to you deplore* (*Twelfth Night 3.1*)

depose VERB if you depose someone you make them take an oath, or swear something to be true ❑ *Depose him in the justice of his cause* (*Richard II 1.3*)

depositary NOUN a depositary is a trustee ❑ *Made you ... my depositary* (*King Lear 2.4*)

derive 1 VERB to derive means to comes from or to descend (it usually applies to people) ❑ *No part of it is mine,/ This shame derives itself from unknown loins.* (*Much Ado About Nothing 4.1*) 2 VERB if you derive something from someone you inherit it ❑ *Treason is not inherited ...Or, if we derive it from our friends/ What's that to me?* (*As You Like It 1.3*)

descry VERB to see or catch sight of ❑ *The news is true, my lord. He is descried* (*Anthony and Cleopatra 3.7*)

desert 1 NOUN desert means worth or merit ❑ *That dost in vile misproson shackle up/ My love and her desert* (*All's Well That Ends Well 2.3*) 2 ADJ desert is used here to mean lonely or isolated ❑ *if that love or gold/ Can in this desert place buy entertainment* (*As You LIke It 2.4*)

design 1 VERB to design means to indicate or point out ❑ *we shall see/ Justice design the victor's chivalry* (*Richard II 1.1*) 2 NOUN a design is a plan, an intention or an undertaking ❑ *hinder not the honour of his design* (*All's Well That Ends Well 3.6*)

designment NOUN a designment was a plan or undertaking ❑ *The desperate tempest hath so bang'd the Turks,/ That their designment halts* (*Othello 2.1*)

despite VERB despite here means to spite or attempt to thwart a plan ❑ *Only to despite them I will endeavour anything* (*Much Ado About Nothing 2.2*)

device NOUN a device is a plan, plot or trick ❑ *Excellent, I smell a device* (*Twelfth Night 2.3*)

disable VERB to disable here means to devalue or make little of ❑ *he disabled my judgement* (*As You Like It 5.4*)

discandy VERB here discandy means to melt away or dissolve ❑ *The hearts ... do discandy , melt their sweets* (*Anthony and Cleopatra 4.12*)

disciple VERB to disciple is to teach or train ❑ *He ...was/ Discipled of the bravest* (*All's Well That Ends Well 1.2*)

discommend VERB if you discommend something you criticize it ❑ *my dialect which you discommend so much* (*King Lear 2.2*)

discourse NOUN discourse means conversation, talk or chat ❑ *which part of it I'll waste/ With such discourse as I not doubt shall make it/ Go quick away* (*The Tempest 5.1*)

discover VERB discover used to mean to reveal or show ❑ *the Prince discovered to Claudio that he loved my niece* (*Much Ado About Nothing 1.2*)

disliken VERB disguise, make unlike ❑ *disliken/ The truth of your own seeming* (*The Winter's Tale 4.4*)

dismantle VERB to dismantle is to remove or take away ❑ *Commit a thing so monstrous to dismantle/*

So many folds of favour (*King Lear* 1.1)

disponge VERB disponge means to pour out or rain down ❑ *The poisonous damp of night disponge upon me* (*Anthony and Cleopatra* 4.9)

distrain VERB to distrain something is to confiscate it ❑ *My father's goods are all distrained and sold* (*Richard II* 2.3)

divers ADJ divers is an old word for various ❑ *I will give out divers schedules of my beauty* (*Twelfth Night* 1.5)

doff VERB to doff is to get rid of or dispose ❑ *make our women fight/ To doff their dire distresses* (*Macbeth* 4.3)

dog VERB if you dog someone or something you follow them or it closely ❑ *I will rather leave to see Hector than not to dog him* (*Troilus and Cressida* 5.1)

dotage NOUN dotage here means infatuation ❑ *Her dotage now I do begin to pity* (*A Midsummer NIght's Dream* 4.1)

dotard NOUN a dotard was an old fool ❑ *I speak not like a dotard nor a fool* (*Much Ado About Nothing* 5.1)

dote VERB to dote is to love, cherish, care without seeing any fault ❑ *And won her soul; and she, sweet lady, dotes,/ Devoutly dotes, dotes in idolatry* (*A Midsummer Night's Dream* 1.1)

doublet NOUN a doublet was a man's close-fitting jacket with short skirt ❑ *Lord Hamlet, with his doublet all unbraced* (*Hamlet* 2.1)

dowager NOUN a dowager is a widow ❑ *Like to a step-dame or a dowage* (*A Midsummer Night's Dream* 1.1)

dowdy NOUN a dowdy was an ugly woman ❑ *Dido was a dowdy* (*Romeo and Juliet* 2.4)

dower NOUN a dower (or dowery) is the riches or property given by the father of a bride to her husband-to-be ❑ *Thy truth then by they dower* (*King Lear* 1.1)

dram NOUN a dram is a tiny amount ❑ *Why, everything adheres together that no dram of a scruple* (*Twelfth Night* 3.4)

drift NOUN drift is a plan, scheme or intention ❑ *Shall Romeo by my letters know our drift* (*Romeo and Juliet* 4.1)

dropsied ADJ dropsied means pretentious ❑ *Where great additions swell's and virtues none/ It is a dropsied honour* (*All's Well That Ends Well* 2.3)

drudge NOUN a drudge was a slave, servant ❑ *If I be his cuckold, he's my drudge* (*All's Well That Ends Well* 1.3)

dwell VERB to dwell sometimes meant to exist, to be ❑ *I'd rather dwell in my necessity* (*Merchant of Venice* 1.3)

earnest ADJ an earnest was a pledge to pay or a payment in advance ❑ *for an earnest of a greater honour/ He bade me from him call thee Thane of Cawdor* (*Macbeth* 1.3)

ecstasy NOUN madness ❑ *This is the very ecstasy of love* (*Hamlet* 2.1)

edict NOUN law or declaration ❑ *It stands as an edict in destiny.* (*A Midsummer Night's Dream* 1.1)

egall ADJ egall is an old word meaning equal ❏ *companions/Whose souls do bear an egall yoke of love* (*Merchant of Venice 2.4*)

eisel NOUN eisel meant vinegar ❏ *Woo't drink up eisel?* (*Hamlet 5.1*)

eke, eke out VERB eke meant to add to, to increase. Eke out nowadays means to make something last as long as possible – particularly in the sense of making money last a long time ❏ *Still be kind/And eke out our performance with your mind* (*Henry V Chorus*)

elbow, out at PHRASE out at elbow is an old phrase meaning in poor condition – as when your jacket sleeves are worn at the elbow which shows that it is an old jacket ❏ *He cannot, sir. He's out at elbow* (*Measure for Measure 2.1*)

element NOUN elements were thought to be the things from which all things were made. They were: air, earth, water and fire ❏ *Does not our lives consist of the four elements?* (*Twelfth Night 2.3*)

elf VERB to elf was to tangle ❏ *I'll ... elf all my hairs in knots* (*King Lear 2.3*)

embassy NOUN an embassy was a message ❏ *We'll once more hear Orsino's embassy.* (*Twelfth Night 1.5*)

emphasis NOUN emphasis here means a forceful expression or strong statement ❏ *What is he whose grief/Bears such an emphasis* (*Hamlet 5.1*)

empiric NOUN an empiric was an untrained doctor sometimes called a quack ❏ *we must not ... prostitute our past-cure malady/To empirics* (*All's Well That Ends Well 2.1*)

emulate ADJ emulate here means envious ❏ *pricked on by a most emulate pride* (*Hamlet 1.1*)

enchant VERB to enchant meant to put a magic spell on ❏ *Damn'd as thou art, thou hast enchanted her,/For I'll refer me to all things of sense* (*Othello 1.2*)

enclog VERB to enclog was to hinder something or to provide an obstacle to it ❏ *Traitors enscarped to enclog the guitless keel* (*Othello 1.2*)

endure VERB to endure was to allow or to permit ❏ *and will endure/Our setting down before't.* (*Macbeth 5.4*)

enfranchise VERB if you enfranchised something you set it free ❏ *Do this or this;/Take in that kingdom and enfranchise that;/Perform't, or else we damn thee.'* (*Anthony and Cleopatra 1.1*)

engage VERB to engage here means to pledge or to promise ❏ *This to be true I do engage my life* (*As You Like It 5.4*)

engaol VERB to lock up or put in prison ❏ *Within my mouth you have engaoled my tongue* (*Richard II 1.3*)

engine NOUN an engine was a plot, device or a machine ❏ *their promises, enticements, oaths, tokens, and all these engines, of lust, are not the things they go under* (*All's Well That Ends Well 3.5*)

englut VERB if you were engulfed you were swallowed up or eaten whole ❏ *For certainly thou art so near the gulf,/Thou needs must be englutted.* (*Henry V 4.3*)

enjoined ADJ enjoined describes people joined together for the same reason ❏ *Of enjoined penitents/*

There's four or five (*All's Well That Ends Well* 3.5)

entertain 1 VERB to entertain here means to welcome or receive ❑ *Approach, rich Ceres, her to entertain.* (*The Tempest* 4.1) 2 VERB to entertain in this context means to cherish, hold in high regard or to respect ❑ *and I quake,/ Lest thou a feverous life shouldst entertain/ And six or seven winters more respect/ Than a perpetual honour.* (*Measure for Measure* 3.1) 3 VERB to entertain means here to give something consideration ❑ *But entertain it,/ And though you think me poor, I am the man/ Will give thee all the world.* (*Anthony and Cleopatra* 2.7) 4 VERB to entertain here means to treat or handle ❑ *your highness is not entertained with that ceremonious affection as you were wont* (*King Lear* 1.4)

envious ADJ envious meant spiteful or vindictive ❑ *he shall appear to the envious a scholar* (*Measure for Measure* 3.2)

ere PREP ere was a common word for before ❑ *ere this I should ha' fatted all the region kites* (*Hamlet* 2.2)

err VERB to err means to go astray, to make a mistake ❑ *And as he errs, doting on Hermia's eyes* (*A Midsummer Night's Dream* 1.1)

erst ADV erst was a common word for once or before ❑ *that erst brought sweetly forth/ The freckled cowslip* (*Henry V* 5.2)

eschew VERB if you eschew something you deliberately avoid doing it ❑ *What cannot be eschewed must be embraced* (*The Merry Wives of Windsor* 5.5)

escote VERB to escote meant to pay for, support ❑ *How are they escoted?* (*Hamlet* 2.2)

estimable ADJ estimable meant appreciative ❑ *I could not with such estimable wonder over-far believe that* (*Twelfth Night* 2.1)

extenuate VERB extenuate means to lessen ❑ *Which by no means we may extenuate* (*A Midsummer Night's Dream* 1.1)

fain ADV fain was a common word meaning gladly or willingly ❑ *I would fain prove so* (*Hamlet* 2.2)

fall NOUN in a voice or music fall meant going higher and lower ❑ *and so die/ That strain again! it had a dying fall* (*Twelfth Night* 1.1)

false ADJ false was a common word for treacherous ❑ *this is counter, you false Danish dogs!* (*Hamlet* 4.5)

fare VERB fare means to get on or manage ❑ *I fare well* (*The Taming of the Shrew Introduction* 2)

feign VERB to feign was to make up, pretend or fake ❑ *It is the more like to be feigned* (*Twelfth Night* 1.5)

fie EXCLAM fie was an exclamation of disgust ❑ *Fie, that you'll say so!* (*Twelfth Night* 1.3)

figure VERB to figure was to symbolize or look like ❑ *Wings and no eyes, figure unheedy haste* (*A Midsummer Night's Dream* 1.1)

filch VERB if you filch something you steal it ❑ *With cunning hast thou filch'd my daughter's heart* (*A Midsummer Night's Dream* 1.1)

flout VERB to flout something meant to scorn it ❑ *Why will you suffer her to flout me thus?* (*A Midsummer Night's Dream* 3.2)

fond ADJ fond was a common word meaning foolish ❑ *Shall we their fond pageant see?* (*A Midsummer Night's Dream 3.2*)

footing 1 NOUN footing meant landing on shore, arrival, disembarkation ❑ *Whose footing here anticipates our thoughts/A se'nnight's speed.* (*Othello 2.1*) 2 NOUN footing also means support ❑ *there your charity would have lacked footing* (*Winter's Tale 3.3*)

forsooth ADV in truth, certainly, truly
❑ *I had rather, forsooth, go before you like a man* (*The Merry Wives of Windsor 3.2*)

forswear VERB if you forswear you lie, swear falsely or break your word ❑ *he swore a thing to me on Monday night, which he forswore on Tuesday morning* (*Much Ado About Nothing 5.1*)

freshes NOUN a fresh is a fresh water stream ❑ *He shall drink nought brine, for I'll not show him/Where the quick freshes are.* (*Tempest 3.2*)

furlong NOUN a furlong is a measure of distance. It is the equivalent on one eight of a mile ❑ *Now would I give a thousand furlongs of sea for an acre of barren ground* (*Tempest 1.1*)

gaberdine NOUN a gaberdine is a cloak ❑ *My best way is to creep under his gaberdine* (*Tempest 2.2*)

gage NOUN a gage was a challenge to duel or fight ❑ *There is my gage, Aumerle, in gage to thine* (*Richard II 4.1*)

gait NOUN your gait is your way of walking or step ❑ *I know her by her gait* (*Tempest 4.1*)

gall VERB to gall is to annoy or irritate ❑ *Let it not gall your patience, good Iago,/That I extend my manners* (*Othello 2.1*)

gambol NOUN frolic or play ❑ *Hop in his walks, and gambol in his eyes* (*A Midsummer Night's Dream 3.1*)

gaskins NOUN gaskins is an old word for trousers ❑ *or, if both break, your gaskins fall.* (*Twelfth Night 1.5*)

gentle ADJ gentle means noble or well-born ❑ *thrice-gentle Cassio!* (*Othello 3.4*)

glass NOUN a glass was another word for a mirror ❑ *no woman's face remember/Save from my glass, mine own* (*Tempest 3.1*)

gleek VERB to gleek means to make a joke or jibe ❑ *Nay, I can gleek upon occasion* (*A Midsummer Night's Dream 3.1*)

gust NOUN gust meant taste, desire or enjoyment. We still say that if you do something with gusto you do it with enjoyment or enthusiasm ❑ *the gust he hath in quarrelling* (*Twelfth Night 1.3*)

habit NOUN habit means clothes ❑ *You know me by my habit* (*Henry V 3.6*)

heaviness NOUN heaviness means sadness or grief ❑ *So sorrow's heaviness doth heavier grow/For debt that bankrupt sleep doth sorrow owe* (*A Midsummer Night's Dream 3.2*)

heavy ADJ if you are heavy you are said to be sad or sorrowful ❑ *Away from light steals home my heavy son* (*Romeo and Juliet 1.1*)

hie VERB to hie meant to hurry ❑ *My husband hies him home* (*All Well That Ends Well 4.4*)

hollowly ADV if you did something hollowly you did it insincerely ❑ *If hollowly invert/What best is boded me to mischief!* (*Tempest 3.1*)

holy-water, court PHRASE if you court holy water you make empty promises, or make statements which sound good but have no real meaning ❑ *court holy-water in a dry house is better than this rain-water out o'door* (*King Lear 3.2*)

howsoever ADV howsoever was often used instead of however ❑ *But howsoever strange and admirable* (*A Midsummer Night's Dream 5.1*)

humour NOUN your humour was your mood, frame of mind or temperament ❑ *it fits my humour well* (*As You Like It 3.2*)

ill ADJ ill means bad ❑ *I must thank him only,/Let my remembrance suffer ill report* (*Antony and Cleopatra 2.2*)

indistinct ADJ inseparable or unable to see a difference ❑ *Even till we make the main and the aerial blue/An indistinct regard.* (*Othello 2.1*)

indulgence NOUN indulgence meant approval ❑ *As you from crimes would pardoned be,/Let your indulgence set me free* (*The Tempest Epilogue*)

infirmity NOUN infirmity was weakness or fraility ❑ *Be not disturbed with my infirmity* (*The Tempest 4.1*)

intelligence NOUN here intelligence means information ❑ *Pursue her; and for this intelligence/If I have thanks* (*A Midsummer Night's Dream 1.1*)

inwards NOUN inwards meant someone's internal organs ❑ *the thought whereof/Doth like a poisonous mineral gnaw my inwards* (*Othello 2.1*)

issue 1 NOUN the issue of a marriage are the children ❑ *To thine and Albany's issues,/Be this perpetual* (*King Lear 1.1*) 2 NOUN in this context issue means outcome or result ❑ *I am to pray you, not to strain my speech,/To grosser issues* (*Othello*)

kind NOUN kind here means situation or case ❑ *But in this kind, wanting your father's voice,/The other must be held the worthier.* (*A Midsummer Night's Dream 1.1*)

knave NOUN a knave was a common word for scoundrel ❑ *How absolute the knave is!* (*Hamlet 5.1*)

league NOUN A distance. A league was the distance a person could walk in one hour ❑ *From Athens is her house remote seven leagues* (*A Midsummer Night's Dream 1.1*)

lief, had as ADJ I had as lief means I should like just as much ❑ *I had as lief the town crier spoke my lines* (*Hamlet 1.2*)

livery NOUN livery was a costume, outfit, uniform usually worn by a servant ❑ *You can endure the livery of a nun* (*A Midsummer Night's Dream 1.1*)

loam NOUN loam is soil containing decayed vegetable matter and therefore good for growing crops and plants ❑ *and let him have some plaster, or some loam, or some rough-cast about him, to signify wall* (*A Midsummer Night's Dream 3.1*)

lusty ADJ lusty meant strong ❑ *and oared/Himself with his good arms in lusty stroke/To th' shore* (*The Tempest 2.1*)

maidenhead NOUN maidenhead means chastity or virginity ❑ *What I am, and what I would, are as secret as maidenhead* (*Twelfth Night 1.5*)

mark VERB mark means to note or pay attention to ❑ *Where sighs and groans,/ Are made not marked* (*Macbeth 4.3*)

marvellous ADJ very or extremely ❑ *here's a marvellous convenient place for our rehearsal* (*A Midsummer Night's Dream 3.1*)

meet ADJ right or proper ❑ *tis most meet you should* (*Macbeth 5.1*)

merely ADV completely or entirely ❑ *Love is merely a madness* (*As You Like It 3.2*)

misgraffed ADJ misgraffed is an old word for mismatched or unequal ❑ *Or else misgraffed in respect of years* (*A Midsummer Night's Dream 1.1*)

misprision NOUN a misprision meant an error or mistake ❑ *Misprision in the highest degree!* (*Twelfth Night 1.5*)

mollification NOUN mollification is appeasement or a way of preventing someone getting angry ❑ *I am to hull here a little longer. Some mollification for your giant* (*Twelfth Night 1.5*)

mouth, cold in the PHRASE a well-known saying of the time which meant to be dead ❑ *What, must our mouths be cold?* (*The Tempest 1.1*)

murmur NOUN murmur was another word for rumour or hearsay ❑ *and then 'twas fresh in murmur* (*Twelfth Night 1.2*)

murrain NOUN murrain was another word for plague, pestilence ❑ *A murrain on your monster, and*

the devil take your fingers! (*The Tempest 3.2*)

neaf NOUN neaf meant fist ❑ *Give me your neaf, Monsieur Mustardseed* (*A Midsummer Night's Dream 4.1*)

nice 1 ADJ nice had a number of meanings here it means fussy or particular ❑ *An therefore, goaded with most sharp occasions,/ Which lay nice manners by, I put you to/ The use of your own virtues* (*All's Well That Ends Well 5.1*) 2 ADJ nice here means critical or delicate ❑ *We're good… To set so rich a man/ On the nice hazard of one doubtful hour?* (*Henry IV part 1*) 3 ADJ nice in this context means carefully accurate, fastidious ❑ *O relation/ Too nice and yet too true!* (*Macbeth 4.3*) 4 ADJ trivial, unimportant ❑ *Romeo .. Bid him bethink/ How nice the quarrel was* (*Romeo and Juliet 3.1*)

nonpareil NOUN if you are nonpareil you are without equal, peerless ❑ *though you were crown'd/ The nonpareil of beauty!* (*Twelfth Night 1.5*)

office NOUN office here means business or work ❑ *Speak your office* (*Twelfth Night 1.5*)

outsport VERB outsport meant to overdo ❑ *Let's teach ourselves that honorable stop,/ Not to outsport discretion.* (*Othello 2.2*)

owe VERB owe meant own, possess ❑ *Lend less than thou owest* (*King Lear 1.4*)

paragon 1 VERB to paragon was to surpass or excede ❑ *he hath achieved a maid/ That paragons description and wild fame* (*Othello 2.1*) 2 VERB to paragon could also mean to compare with ❑ *I will give thee* *bloody teeth If thou with Caesar paragon again/My man of men (Anthony and Cleopatra 1.5)*

pate NOUN pate is another word for head ❑ *Back, slave, or I will break thy pate across* (*The Comedy of Errors 2.1*)

paunch VERB to paunch someone is to stab (usually in the stomach). Paunch is still a common word for a stomach ❑ *Batter his skull, or paunch him with a stake* (*The Tempest 3.2*)

peevish ADJ if you are peevish you are irritable or easily angered ❑ *Run after that same peevish messenger* (*Twelfth Night 1.5*)

peradventure ADV perhaps or maybe ❑ *Peradventure this is not Fortune's work* (*As You Like It 1.2*)

perforce 1 ADV by force or violently ❑ *my rights and royalties,/Plucked from my arms perforce* (*Richard II 2.3*) 2 ADV necessarily ❑ *The hearts of men, they must perforce have melted* (*Richard II 5.2*)

personage NOUN personage meant your appearance ❑ *Of what personage and years is he?* (*Twelfth Night 1.5*)

pestilence NOUN pestilence was a common word for plague or disease ❑ *Methought she purg'd the air of pestilence!* (*Twelfth Night 1.1*)

physic NOUN physic was medicine or a treatment ❑ *tis a physic/That's bitter to sweet end* (*Measure for Measure 4.6*)

place NOUN place means a person's position or rank ❑ *Sons, kinsmen, thanes,/And you whose places are the nearest* (*Macbeth 1.4*)

post NOUN here a post means a messenger ❑ *there are twenty weak and wearied posts/Come from the north* (*Henry IV part II 2.4*)

pox NOUN pox was a word for any disease during which the victim had blisters on the skin. It was also a curse, a swear word ❑ *The pox of such antic, lisping, affecting phantasims* (*Romeo and Juliet 2.4*)

prate VERB to prate means to chatter ❑ *if thou prate of mountains* (*Hamlet 5.1*)

prattle VERB to prattle is to chatter or talk without purpose ❑ *I prattle out of fashion, and I dote In mine own comforts* (*Othello 2.1*)

precept NOUN a precept was an order or command ❑ *and my father's precepts I therein do forget.* (*The Tempest 3.1*)

present ADJ present here means immediate ❑ *We'll put the matter to the present push* (*Hamlet 5.1*)

prithee EXCLAM prithee is the equivalent of please or may I ask – a polite request ❑ *I prithee, and I'll pay thee bounteously* (*Twelfth Night 1.2*)

prodigal NOUN a prodigal is someone who wastes or squanders money ❑ *he's a very fool, and a prodigal* (*Twelfth Night 1.3*)

purpose NOUN purpose is used here to mean intention ❑ *understand my purposes aright* (*King Lear 1.4*)

quaff VERB quaff was a common word which meant to drink heavily or take a big drink ❑ *That quaffing and drinking will undo you* (*Twelfth Night 1.3*)

quaint 1 ADJ clever, ingenious ❑ *with a quaint device* (*The Tempest 3.3*) 2 ADJ cunning ❑ *I'll... tell quaint lies* (*Merchant of Venice 3.4*) 3 ADJ pretty, attractive ❑ *The clamorous owl, that nightly hoots and wonders/At our quaint spirit* (*A Midsummer Night's Dream 2.2*)

quoth VERB an old word which means say ❑ *'Tis dinner time.' quoth I* (*The Comedy of Errors 2.1*)

rack NOUN a rack described clouds or a cloud formation ❑ *And, like this insubstantial pageant faded,/ Leave not a rack behind* (*The Tempest 4.1*)

rail VERB to rant or swear at. It is still used occasionally today ❑ *Why do I rail on thee* (*Richard II 5.5*)

rate NOUN rate meant estimate, opinion ❑ *My son is lost, and, in my rate, she too* (*The Tempest 2.1*)

recreant NOUN recreant is an old word which means coward ❑ *Come, recreant, come, thou child* (*A Midsummer Night's Dream 3.2*)

remembrance NOUN remembrance is used here to mean memory or recollection ❑ *our remembrances of days foregone* (*All's Well That Ends Well 1.3*)

resolute ADJ firm or not going to change your mind ❑ *You are resolute, then?* (*Twelfth Night 1.5*)

revels NOUN revels means celebrations or a party ❑ *Our revels now are ended* (*The Tempest 4.1*)

rough-cast NOUN a mixture of lime and gravel (sometimes shells too) for use on an outer wall ❑ *and let him have some plaster, or some loam, or some rough-cast about him, to signify wall* (*A Midsummer Night's Dream 3.1*)

sack NOUN sack was another word for wine ❑ *My man-monster hath drowned his tongue in sack.* (*The Tempest 3.2*)

sad ADJ in this context sad means serious, grave ❑ *comes me the Prince and Claudio... in sad conference* (*Much Ado About Nothing 1.3*)

sampler NOUN a piece of embroidery, which often showed the family tree ❑ *Both on one sampler, sitting on one cushion* (*A Midsummer Night's Dream 3.2*)

saucy ADJ saucy means rude ❑ *I heard you were saucy at my gates* (*Twelfth Night 1.5*)

schooling NOUN schooling means advice ❑ *I have some private schooling for you both.* (*A Midsummer Night's Dream 1.1*)

seething ADJ seething in this case means boiling – we now use seething when we are very angry ❑ *Lovers and madmen have such seething brains* (*A Midsummer Night's Dream 5.1*)

semblative ADJ semblative means resembling or looking like ❑ *And all is semblative a woman's part.* (*Twelfth Night 1.4*)

several ADJ several here means separate or different ❑ *twenty several messengers* (*Anthony and Cleopatra 1.5*)

shrew NOUN An annoying person or someone who makes you cross ❑ *Bless you, fair shrew.* (*Twelfth Night 1.3*)

shroud VERB to shroud is to hide or shelter ❏ *I will here, shroud till the dregs of the storm be past* (*The Tempest 2.2*)

sickleman NOUN a sickleman was someone who used a sickle to harvest crops ❏ *You sunburnt sicklemen, of August weary* (*The Tempest 4.1*)

soft ADV soft here means wait a moment or stop ❏ *But, soft, what nymphs are these* (*A Midsummer Night's Dream 4.1*)

something ADV something here means somewhat or rather ❏ *Be something scanter of your maiden presence* (*Hamlet 1.3*)

sooth NOUN truly ❏ *Yes, sooth; and so do you* (*A Midsummer Night's Dream 3.2*)

spleen NOUN spleen means fury or anger ❏ *That, in a spleen, unfolds both heaven and earth* (*A Midsummer Night's Dream 1.1*)

sport NOUN sport means recreation or entertainment ❏ *I see our wars/ Will turn unto a peaceful comic sport* (*Henry VI part I 2.2*)

strain NOUN a strain is a tune or a musical phrase ❏ *and so die/That strain again! it had a dying fall* (*Twelfth Night 1.1*)

suffer VERB in this context suffer means perish or die ❏ *but an islander that hath lately suffered by a thunderbolt.* (*The Tempest 2.2*)

suit NOUN a suit is a petition, request or proposal (marriage) ❏ *Because she will admit no kind of suit* (*Twelfth Night 1.2*)

sup VERB to sup is to have supper ❏ *Go know of Cassio where he supped tonight* (*Othello 5.1*)

surfeit NOUN a surfeit is an amount which is too large ❏ *If music be the food of love, play on;/Give me excess of it, that, surfeiting,/ The appetite may sicken* (*Twelfth Night 1.1*)

swain NOUN a swain is a suitor or person who wants to marry ❏ *take this transformed scalp/From off the head of this Athenian swain* (*A Midsummer Night's Dream 4.1*)

thereto ADV thereto meant also ❏ *If she be black, and thereto have a wit* (*Othello 2.1*)

throstle NOUN a throstle was a name for a song-bird ❏ *The throstle with his note so true* (*A Midsummer Night's Dream 3.1*)

tidings NOUN tidings meant news ❏ *that upon certain tidings now arrived, importing the mere perdition of the Turkish fleet* (*Othello 2.2*)

transgress VERB if you transgress you break a moral law or rule of behaviour ❏ *Virtue that transgresses is but patched with sin* (*Twelfth Night 1.5*)

troth, by my PHRASE this phrase means I swear or in truth or on my word ❏ *By my troth, Sir Toby, you must come in earlier o' nights* (*Twelfth Night 1.3*)

trumpery NOUN trumpery means things that look expensive but are worth nothing (often clothing) ❏ *The trumpery in my house, go bring it hither/For stale catch these thieves* (*The Tempest 4.1*)

twink NOUN In the wink of an eye or no time at all ❏ *Ay, with a twink* (*The Tempest 4.1*)

undone ADJ if something or someone is undone they are ruined, destroyed, brought down ❑ *You have undone a man of fourscore three* (*The Winter's Tale 4.4*)

varlets NOUN varlets were villains or ruffians ❑ *Say again: where didst thou leave these varlets?* (*The Tempest 4.1*)

vaward NOUN the vaward is an old word for the vanguard, front part or earliest ❑ *And since we have the vaward of the day* (*A Midsummer Night's Dream 4.1*)

visage NOUN face ❑ *when Phoebe doth behold/Her silver visage in the watery glass* (*A Midsummer Night's Dream 1.1*)

voice NOUN voice means vote ❑ *He has our voices* (*Coriolanus 2.3*)

waggish ADJ waggish means playful ❑ *As waggish boys in game themselves forswear* (*A Midsummer Night's Dream 1.1*)

wane VERB to wane is to vanish, go down or get slighter. It is most often used to describe a phase of the moon ❑ *but, O, methinks, how slow/This old moon wanes* (*A Midsummer Night's Dream 1.1*)

want VERB to want means to lack or to be without ❑ *a beast that wants discourse of reason/Would have mourned longer* (*Hamlet 1.2*)

warrant VERB to assure, promise, guarantee ❑ *I warrant your grace* (*As You Like It 1.2*)

welkin NOUN welkin is an old word for the sky or the heavens ❑ *The starry welkin cover thou anon/With drooping fog as black as Acheron* (*A Midsummer Night's Dream 3.2*)

wench NOUN wench is an old word for a girl ❑ *Well demanded, wench* (*The Tempest 1.2*)

whence ADV from where ❑ *Whence came you, sir?* (*Twelfth Night 1.5*)

wherefore ADV why ❑ *Wherefore, sweetheart? what's your metaphor?* (*Twelfth Night 1.3*)

wide-chopped ADJ if you were wide-chopped you were big-mouthed ❑ *This wide-chopped rascal* (*The Tempest 1.1*)

wight NOUN wight is an old word for person or human being ❑ *She was a wight, if ever such wight were* (*Othello 2.1*)

wit NOUN wit means intelligence or wisdom ❑ *thou didst conclude hairy men plain dealers, without wit* (*The Comedy of Errors 2.2*)

wits NOUN wits mean mental sharpness ❑ *we that have good wits have much to answer for* (*As You Like It 4.1*)

wont ADJ to wont is to be in the habit of doing something regularly ❑ *When were you wont to use my sister thus?* (*The Comedy of Errors 2.2*)

wooer NOUN a wooer is a suitor, someone who is hoping to marry ❑ *and of a foolish knight that you brought in one night here to be her wooer* (*Twelfth Night 1.3*)

wot VERB wot is an old word which means know or learn ❑ *for well I wot/Thou runnest before me* (*A Midsummer Night's Dream 3.2*)